Prologue

Percival Pranworthy, junior solicitor at Beavis and McBeavis of Mayfair, London, was not happy. He was breathing out in exasperated gulps and puffing up his plump cheeks, which were now turning crimson with rage.

Percival had heard blood-curdling tales about the island, of packs of wolves. Some people had even said they were not wolves but werewolves, who had leapt into moving carriages and dragged passengers out of the windows. The passengers were never seen again. He had heard of highwaymen robbing people. And, if that wasn't enough, he'd heard of bloodsucking vampire bats and weird zombie locals too.

When he had flattened out one of the crumpled pages of the newspaper with one of his pink, manicured hands, he continued to read a witness's account. While scanning through it Percival pulled a face in derision, and tutted as he read each sentence. He, of course, found all these stories hard to take seriously. He was not in the least bit frightened, more like annoyed that he had been ordered to go to this primitive place in the first place …

Huh. Werewolves, indeed. As if.

Percival Pranworthy, the only son of the Honourable Pranworthys of Astersley House, Cheshire, had expected to do nothing more than make notes on a couple of wills, hand them over to his superiors, and then go home. How wrong was he? He wasn't a qualified solicitor, but his parents had paid a huge sum to the practice for him to work at Beavis and McBeavis. But now he had to take the place of his overbearing, nasal-voiced employer, Mr Ronald Beavis, to go to the McFetrich estate to meet some reclusive client who wanted to make a will. Mr Beavis had said he had to go to a family wedding in Truro, but the name of the bridegroom was one Percival had never heard him mention before.

Huh. I'm sure he made it up so he didn't have to deal with the estate of Remus McFetrich, thought Percival, pursing his lips angrily. It was so unfair. Why should he have to deal with the McFetrich estate? Why couldn't they send Ronald's pet instead? This was drippy, Cedric Panders – a porridge-faced, bandy-legged junior solicitor working at Beavis and McBeavis.

After smoothing his gingery-brown winged hair he took out a small mirror and re-examined his sparse beard and mutton-chop sideburns. The face peering back from the mirror was shaped like a pudding basin, with narrow, monkey-brown eyes. His nose was long, with a warty bump on the bridge. He had a thin slit for a mouth, which was getting lost in a fast-developing double chin. Not a pleasant face. It appeared to have a permanent sneer. Stocky, some would say chubby. At barely five feet six, he tended to wear lifts in his leather boots to give the impression of extra height.

The long journey to Oban had been bad enough and his overnight stay at the bed and breakfast, run in his opinion by a short-tempered harridan of a woman with smelly, eggy breath, had made it seem worse. Then he had had to travel in a filthy boat the next day to Howly Island in very choppy seas. At one point he thought it would capsize because of a black mass under the swirling waters – believed by the terrified boatman to be a sea monster, of all things.

Percival had not even seen it, so he thought the boatman was just trying to frighten him. Having said that, the esteemed Marchioness of Bute had told him about a mysterious black cat seen swimming off the coast of Bute. It was a friend of the cruel mermaids of the Black Sea, and was believed to have been responsible for numerous shipwrecks in those waters. The giant cat was, according to hearsay, a monster of a creature, jet-black with long, curved claws and glittering yellow eyes that swallowed trading ships whole. Percival could not believe that the Marchioness, someone of such importance, would believe anything that was rubbish, so the story must surely have been true.

Leaving the bed and breakfast had, in his opinion, been the start of an atrocious day. The shabbily dressed carriage driver had dripped rainwater on his cloak after getting soaking wet repairing one of the

Stevie Rump and the Werewolves of Howly Island

By

Amber A. Cross

ISBN: 978-0-244-33694-3

www.publishnation.co.uk

huge wheels of the carriage, and had drenched Percival further when he gave him some refreshment. Instead of apologising the insolent man had said it couldn't be helped, due to the torrential rain.

Now, on the road to Banmorach, leading to Loch House, the uneven road was making the carriage jolt up and down and causing him to feel quite sick. He placed one of his hands in his right coat pocket and took out a small black leather case. It contained a jewel-encrusted gold fob watch. He saw that he was behind time and would be late getting to the McFetrich estate.

"I bet he's doing this deliberately," he fumed, and placed the black case back in his pocket. If there was one thing he could not tolerate that was rudeness from the lower classes.

Half a mile down the road to Loch House, with the carriage bobbing up and down in its stomach-churning way, furious Percival tapped on the window with his cane.

"You are steering the horses like a maniac, fool. Slow down."

The driver, hearing this, stopped the carriage with a sudden jolt so that Percival fell forward.

"Right. I have had enough," he shouted, finally losing his temper over Percival's horrible behaviour. "That's it, laddie. You can get oot. I have had enough of your rudeness. I can do without toffs speaking to me like you. I dinna have ta put up with this. Go on. Get oot. That's it. Get oot."

"How dare you speak to me like that, you ignorant buffoon! I will have you sacked. I demand you take me to Loch House this instant. I most certainly will not get out of your carriage. Drive on, man, and mind your manners. Know your place."

The carriage driver, a sad-looking man with upturned eyes and frizzy brown hair, stared at Percival for a second then climbed down from his driving seat, opened the carriage door, dragged Percival out by his black frock coat, and threw his leather case after him.

Percival lay on the ground sputtering, his face beetroot with rage, and shouted,

"How dare you! How dare you! I tell you, I will have you sacked. You will never work again by the time I am finished with you."

Turning round the carriage driver stared back at him with tired eyes, which Percival failed to notice. He didn't say anything at first, then gave him a strange look, and said coldly,

"Will you, now? Well, I dinna give a tinker's cuss as they say. All I'll say to you, laddie, is it's a cold and dark night to be walking round here. I would watch out for the werewolves if I were you heh heh." Then, laughing and displaying black teeth, he got back in the driver's seat, turned the carriage round, and began going back down the steep hill.

"Werewolves," shouted Percival. "What did you mean about werewolves?" But it was too late. The carriage driver had gone.

He struggled to get up, then picked up his nut-brown leather case and dusted it down while checking it hadn't been scratched.

"Werewolves. What rubbish. I bet he made it up to frighten me. He will be laughing on the other side of his face when I report him and ensure he never gets a job again. Does he not know who my family are? My father will have him horsewhipped," Percival raged.

As he looked ahead he saw a dirt track that went up towards a hill. To his right was a wild-looking black forest. There was not a soul to be seen. He snorted and decided to walk up the side of the road and flag down a carriage if it came his way. Surely, even in this godforsaken place, carriages came this way. The sky was now ablaze with a blood-red moon, which gave him some light as he walked up the dark road, but the wet ground was littered with clusters of thick lipped black slimy slugs which he had to step over to his utter revulsion.

A thick, long-fingered white mist appeared out of nowhere, enveloping his face and body, and making it difficult to see as he struggled further up the hill. Percival was breathing heavily. His face was now purple, and he was sweating heavily too. He removed a tiny bottle of Green Fern gentleman's cologne from his breast pocket and poured some on to his forehead. Then, as an afterthought, he put some under his sweating armpits.

While he was moaning to himself at his predicament, he lost part of the road he was walking on to a broken carriage. When he peered into it he saw an old abandoned suitcase stretched across the seat. He thought of having a look inside to see if there was something he could take, but was put off by all the extremely large spiders covering the case. So instead he walked on.

To his right he passed oak trees and rowan trees, which annoyed him further as they started to take away some of his light. As he tutted to himself it was only now that he began to feel slightly afraid. Wasn't it a bad sign to be walking in the dark when there was a blood moon? And had he not heard a story about scarecrows coming to life and taking the souls of people?

Oh, this is so ridiculous, he thought. He sounded like one of his father's stupid, uneducated maids. But then he began to worry about something else and bit on the corner of one of his nails nervously. *Hadn't there been talk of robbers on this stretch of road? And why was this carriage abandoned in the middle of the road without the owner even taking his suitcase? What had happened to him?*

There was complete silence, apart from the sound of Percival's leather boot heels scraping along the ground. As he finally got to the top of the hill he saw what he thought might be Loch House in the distance. Relieved, he walked briskly down to it. The forest to his right had started, in his nervous mind, to look quite threatening.

Better to nearly get run over by passing carriages than walk through a forest full of God knows what, he thought, now feeling more confident. But his boots were a tight fit. Why did one boot squeak and not the other? He sighed and was full of self-pity, and was deep in thought when an owl suddenly hooted. While half-jumping in the air with fright, he turned around. Catching sight of the offending creature perched on a branch of a tree he pulled a face at it, then picked up a pebble and threw it at it. It missed the bird, but seeing the bird flap its wings and fly off in fear gave him deep satisfaction.

While he was still smirking to himself a noise made him turn around. Scratching noises appeared to be coming from some thick gorse bushes as he passed them. Something seemed to be raising the bushes, making the leaves shake violently. It then stopped as soon as it had started.

It was then that he heard it.

Something moving behind him.

Heavy breathing.

Then snarling.

A red-hot wetness touched the back of his neck. It felt like his skin had been scraped red raw.

"Ouch! Ouch! Ouch!" he shouted, jumping up and already feeling sore as he rubbed at it. But it wasn't just skin he felt. His fingers felt something else …

Something warm.

Powdery fur.

Then came the smell of wet dog.

Overcome with fear, he went to turn around, but his body was pushed forward. Still screaming loudly, he landed with a thud. On looking up he looked up into the eyes of an enormous blue-eyed black wolf on all fours sitting beside him.

Percival's eyes bulged as he mouthed the word, "Woo … wooo … wolf," gulping and repeating it several times as if unable to believe what he was seeing. The animal did not move. It just stared intently at him.

By this time Percival's body was shaking with fear. He got up and started to move backwards very slowly. The creature moved its gargantuan hairy paws towards him in a crawling motion, and raised its coarse black and grey hunched back in the air. The hair on its face was spiked round its whiskered cheeks. The eyes were of the palest blue, slanted at the corners. It had a short snout, and its red tongue was folded back into its wide mouth. Drops of saliva hung off its chin and dripped silently down. Percival watched them fall on to its deep grey throat and then on to the ground.

The wolf looked at him but made no attempt to come any nearer to him. Then it cocked its head and studied him, and slowly made to move towards him. But then it lifted one of its ears, as if it were hearing something, and flattened its body down on the ground. The whole of its body language had changed. While seizing this opportunity Percival turned around and began to run and run. Faster and faster he ran, something he had never done before. Fear gave him the strength to keep on running as he ran up the hill, not looking back. He gulped air and swallowed a small fly, but on he ran, hardly daring to breathe loudly.

He strained his ears but could hear nothing. There was only the sound of his boots clicking as he ran further and further up the hill. He was now not far from Loch House, and so near he could see it quite clearly. The sketch he had been given of it was extremely accurate. On he ran, further and further, but he then had to stop to catch his breath and could not go any further. His heart felt as if it was fit to burst. Behind him his ears could hear nothing. Relieved, he finally stopped. There was not much further to go. Half-laughing with fear, he felt a terrified relief.

Ha! I have outsmarted a wolf. Wait until I tell the family, he thought, now calming down and smiling to himself. Of course, he would embellish the story. He would say he shot it.

"Yes, that's what I'll say I did." Penelope Masterson, the colonel's daughter, would look up to him then and beg him to marry her. He would make her suffer for keeping him waiting. Maybe he could get someone better than her, after all. She wasn't that perfect: a bit skinny, with her blonde hair that went frizzy in cold weather. He had to admit her high-pitched voice did sometimes grate on him and the annoying way she started a sentence with the words, "I say, Percival," all the time.

As he walked gingerly across slippery, wet stones he had to tread carefully, worried he would fall over. His brand-new boots were now ruined, the heels caked in thick, gooey mud. He was not happy about that. He looked at his boots and sniffed them, and realised that some of it seemed to be dog poo with what looked like a long black hair in the middle of it.

"Oh, this is so horrible. Dog poo ... I have stood in dog poo. Yuck, yuck, yuck. What a horrible smell. My lovely boots ... Ugh ... I think I'm going to be sick. I will wring that horrible stinky dog's neck if I see it," he shouted angrily. Then he tried to scrape the ripe-smelling poo off his boots on the side of the road, without much success. He couldn't let his client see him with his shoes stinking of dog poo. "Oh, this is just too horrible."

Scrape scrape scrape went his boots as he continued trying to clean them by the grass verge. But then he stopped, his vanity taken over by fear. It was too quiet. No birds were singing now. The eerie silence was quickly broken by a howling wind, which surrounded him, along with a strange-smelling mist that made it difficult for him to see. When it cleared he was about to turn around to check he was still well away from the wolf, but then there came a crashing darkness around him. Something had jumped on him and was smothering the life out of him.

He couldn't breathe.

An icy coldness burnt into his cheeks.

Then he saw it. His eyes began to pop out of their sockets. Its dragon breath burnt into his face. Then came more blackness, and he fainted at the horrific sight of what he had come face to face with.

It was just as well he had. The creature dragging him away in its mouth was much larger than the wolf he had encountered. It stood well over six feet tall on its hind legs. The way it walked, stoop-backed, was almost humanlike, and its body was covered in thick, coarse black hair. It began grunting noises to the rest of the pack. Then the werewolf dropped Percival, making a heart-chilling noise as it raised its head back. Its sharp, pointed yellow fangs gleamed in the moonlight as it gave primeval wails, followed by the pack's ear-shattering howls in allegiance. After coming closer they joined their leader and began to tuck into their plump, juicy supper.

What Percival had thought to be dog poo on the heels of his expensive leather boots had in fact been werewolf poo.

So that was the end of poor unfortunate Percival Pranworthy. But this was just the beginning of another adventure for Stevie Rump, Bruce, and Fergal.

Chapter 1

"Fergal's inherited a loch house on an island? C'mon, you gotta be kidding me, Stevie, man," Bruce replied. The mackerel tabby cat was speaking in his strong Caribbean voice and licking butter off his paws as he tucked into his thickly sliced fish toast.

"No, honestly, Bruce, I heard my mum talking about it to Dad. Fergal is the only surviving relative of Remus McFetrich. His uncle apparently turned into a bit of a recluse and cut himself off from all the family. He lived at a loch house on the island and surrounded himself with rare animals. He even had pet pythons," answered Stevie, speaking softly in his English-accented voice, and brushing a stray strand of fair hair out of one of his hazel-coloured eyes.

"Snakes! Snakes ... Jeez, don't mention them to me. Not after what happened to you, man, at the Island of Glendowwer. If it hadn't been for Ethan and his men you would have been a goner. Ugh ... Sure gives me the horrors when I think of them witches," shuddered Bruce, coki-eyed, and wagged his striped tail agitatedly.

The Dog Pirates' leader, Ethan, a Rhodesian ridgeback, had killed a gigantic snake, which had swallowed Stevie whole. Ethan had rescued Stevie, who had been in danger of suffocating, just in time. It was during the time of the Great War of the Witches and Mermaids in the Caribbean.

Bruce shook his head, as if to wipe out the frightening memory. His striped tail was still swishing as he thought more deeply about it. The giant snake had been Edna, the mother of Gledwyn, the evil Sea Witch. She was a shape-shifter who had changed into a snake to eat Stevie and his friends, but by swallowing him whole had not killed him. The snake, when killed, had to be cut open to get Stevie out of its vast stomach.

"I know, Bruce. I know. I still have nightmares about it. You know, I honestly thought I was in a dark tunnel. But I bet there're not many people who can say they were swallowed by an enormous python."

"Yeah, and who lived to tell the tale. So, don't do that to me again, Stevie. I don't think my nine lives could take a fright like that again, and if I see another witch or monster again I think I'll wet myself."

"Oh … Bruce, chill out. It's all over now. All the Sea Witches have been rounded up now. Gledwyn the Witch was banished, if you remember, to the Wailing Planet."

" I know, I know, but I don't think I'll ever be able to forget that. Oh, let's change the subject, man. It's way too scary to think about. Where's Fergal's uncle's island?"

"It's on the West Coast of Scotland. It's called Howly Island. Well, I think that's how it's pronounced. Mum said she thinks it may have been called Holy Island at one time, but the name was dropped for some reason."

"What's that you're talking about, Stevie?" a voice asked from behind them, making Bruce jump.

"Oh, hi, Fergal. We were talking about your island," Stevie replied to the white cormorant as he strutted into the kitchen.

"It's called Howly Island," replied Fergal the cormorant, rather pompously. "I intend to go out there in a couple of days. I just need to tie things up with my solicitor."

"Hey, Fergal, whatever have you got on?" Bruce asked, his mouth turning up in amusement. "You look like that old Bob from the fish quay."

"This is the latest country attire, something I will be wearing from now on. I most certainly do not look like old Bob from the fish quay. This is from Hunt & Holditch, a gentleman's outfitters … something a tomcat would not understand. I had it sent from my tailor's in London. I will be a laird shortly, and locals will expect me to dress more like this." As he spoke he smoothed the snow-white feathers on his head, placed his tweed cap carefully at a right angle on his head, and smiled snootily.

Instead of being offended at Fergal's remark, Bruce continued to tuck into his toast, dripping the remainder of the butter down the soft down of his belly, but now and again he took a sneaky peek at Fergal in his attire in blinding curiosity.

Fergal, the snow-white cormorant with pale blue eyes, was dressed in a thick three-quarter-length grey tweed coat that was belted at the waist. On his two long twig legs were short trousers, puffed up and gathered around the top of his legs. These were held up by gaiters, and his calves were covered in thin diamond-patterned green and black socks. His feet were encased in highly polished black laced-up ankle boots. In his feathered right hand he carried a black silk umbrella.

"What have you got an umbrella for, Fergal? Why, it's baking hot outside," Bruce asked, swallowing his last corner piece of toast a bit too quickly, which caused him to give a slight cough.

"This, Bruce, is not just any umbrella. It's made with the finest woven silks." Fergal twisted the umbrella in his feathered white hand in a dramatic fashion and pointed it at him as if in a duel. "It is to protect me from highwaymen."

"Highwaymen? Around here?" asked Bruce, puzzled and trying not to laugh.

"No, not here, idiot. There has been a spate of robberies on Howly Island. I have been informed about them by my solicitor, Mr Beavis of Beavis and McBeavis. He said I should take something to protect me. The last solicitor who went to the island was robbed by a highwayman and left trussed up on the side of the road. He was lucky to be alive. The solicitor who went before that completely disappeared. It was said he might have been killed by wolves. His body was never found."

"Wolves? Jeez. How did they know it might have been wolves?" Bruce asked, his pale green eyes now enlarged and on stalks.

"Well, they say it might have been wolves. He just disappeared into thin air. Would you believe all they found was a pair of boots, a briefcase, and a very expensive watch?" Fergal shuddered as he spoke.

"Well, in that case, I think you will need more than an umbrella, Fergal," replied Stevie, worriedly.

"Oh, don't worry about me. I also have a pistol in my cloak if I need it. I have been taking shooting lessons and have just recently read *The Baron Charles Ranger de Barony's*, a gentleman's book on how to protect yourself and your property. I am perfectly equipped in the event of ruffians attacking me," responded Fergal airily.

"Are you flying over there?"

"Good heavens, no. I don't fly as much as I used to. That's too much hard work. I will be going by train – first class, of course – followed by steamboat. It will be a strange experience, of course, but my solicitor said a horse and carriage then finally a ferry and a small rowing boat will take me to the island."

"Wow. That sounds like a long journey. Are you sure you will be all right? Bruce replied, sounding worried and seeing the sad look on Fergal's face.

"I should think so," replied Fergal, looking down and sounding not too sure and rather nervous, as the false bravado slipped from his face.

"Hey … We could come with you," said Bruce, earnestly.

"You can forget that. There's no chance of Mum and Dad letting us go. They still haven't recovered after what happened at Glendowwer," came Stevie's quick reply.

"Yeah, yeah, I know. But we could say we're going as companions, to keep him company so he isn't lonely," came Bruce's determined reply. He was not giving in, and was worried about how Fergal would fare on his own without them.

"I'm not going to be alone, you know. I'm going with Mr Beavis, the solicitor, but you two could come with me. I would pay for everything. That's a great idea, thought of by me, of course. Surely your mum and dad would let you go if you said you were travelling with a solicitor."

"I'm not sure. I will have to ask them, Fergal. Now is not the right moment, but don't mention highwaymen to them. If that's mentioned then we have no chance of going there. You two don't say anything to them on that, right?" Stevie pondered it then said, "Since we moved from St Lucia to Edinburgh they have been very busy setting up the new orphanage. Let me see how I get on with asking them. Tell you what, guys, I'll ask them after Queen Victoria's visit to Edinburgh. That's bound to put them in a good mood."

Fergal and Bruce nodded in reply, both excited and hoping that all three of them could go to Howly Island. It sounded like such a cool place.

Chapter 2

It had been a very bad sea journey, coming from St Lucia in the Caribbean and having to sail through shark-infested waters to the new house in Edinburgh. Stevie, Fergal, and Bruce had suffered terrible seasickness. At one point the ship, the *Serpent*, had nearly capsized, because of twenty overenthusiastic mermaids and dolphins rushing to greet Stevie, Bruce, and Fergal; they had gathered quite a fan club in the Caribbean. The mermaids and mermen and the undersea creatures had been eternally grateful to the trio for rescuing Selena, Queen of the Mermaids, from her underwater prison. Selena then went on to conquer the evil Sea Witch Gledwyn during the War of the Mermaids and the Sea Witches, and to free them – adults, children, and marine life – from slavery.

When Bruce, Fergal, and Stevie heard the news from Stevie's parents, Max and Christine Rump, about moving to Craigowan House, Edinburgh, they had been horrified.

"But why move? We love it here," came Stevie's completely baffled reply.

"It was only ever going to be temporary, Stevie – staying in St Lucia, I mean. Caras Minefletcher is a wonderful nun, and she and her sisters have done amazing things for children and orphanages in the past. Now we've set up the orphanage in the Caribbean they will continue the work. We have done all we can now over here. Craigowan House is an old asylum: there are not enough children's homes in Edinburgh. Both your father and I aim to do something about that," said his mother determinedly.

Despite Stevie's endless moaning and saying he would hate Edinburgh, Stevie's mother would not be swayed. The furniture was shipped out, the cases were packed, and they set sail for Edinburgh, Scotland, but not with Phoebe.

Phoebe was an orphan, who had been sold to the Sea Witches of Glendowwer by her evil aunt after her mother died so she could gain Phoebe's inheritance. However, Phoebe had been rescued by Bruce,

Stevie, and Fergal. She now lived in the Rump household. She was to follow with Alice Markham, the new housekeeper. Phoebe, a pretty girl with long straight fair hair, had grown as tall as Stevie. She was pale-faced and had freckles and sparkling blue eyes. Her hair always tied in its trademark tight ponytail. She was now beginning to look at the Rump family as her own family.

Stevie had been worried she would stay at the orphanage. But when he asked his mother, she said,

"Wherever did you get that idea? Why, she is one of the family. Phoebe had to study for her nursing exams, so it was better she came later. I most certainly would not have allowed her to travel on her own, so I asked Alice Markham if she would come back with her."

When she looked at her son she saw a very young-looking hazel-eyed boy with a long thin face and a small snub nose, who was very much like his father, Max. Stevie was lanky, with what his family called his trademark long feet. Because he had not quite yet grown into his height, he could be accident-prone. His shaggy blonde hair had shades of white in it after years spent in the Caribbean, and the fringe part covered his eyes. His skin had been a honey-golden colour, which was quickly fading, and now he had a faint scattering of pale pink spots on his chin.

The new house, Craigowan House, was quite austere. It was one of Edinburgh's old, crumbling orphanages. The house was grey-fronted hewn ashlar. Four stories high, it was surrounded by rusted iron railings with yellow and green clumps of weeds growing in between them. It seemed to carry an air of sadness about it. It was reputed to be haunted by the ghosts of orphans who had been ill-treated. No dogs would enter the premises, which was something that was a relief to Bruce.

Stevie, Bruce, and Fergal had found it difficult to cope with all the cold weather in Edinburgh. Today had been a one-off day. There was bright sunshine. It seemed as Stevie, Fergal, and Bruce would never take their jumpers off. What with the thick fog and rain, Stevie wondered if Edinburgh ever had a dry day. Even Bruce had been cold, and had taken to wearing one of Fergal's old light blue jumpers. The locals also found it difficult to understand Bruce's

Caribbean accent, and Bruce tended to have to repeat what he said to them. But the excitement of the upcoming royal visit had started to take their minds off the disappointing move.

Bruce had never been so excited. He had been making a special cranachan trifle for Queen Victoria. The huge white trifle was made with oatmeal, double cream, runny honey, and blackberries. Bruce then placed a delicate white crown to fit on top of it. Red and green sugared pearls covered the top in all their festooned glory. Even Fergal, who had been a chef, was impressed, and told him it was truly fit for a queen.

The trifle was made in a red-rimmed pressed glass dish. The inside of the dish was engraved with glass roses, and the petals were slightly raised to give it a regal effect. It was then placed in a large wicker basket with a white cloth to cover it.

Queen Victoria's visit was going to take place on 28 September 1842. She was to unveil a statue of her late father. The Duke of Buccleuch was then to lead her to Edinburgh Castle. Prince Albert was to accompany her on this visit. It was a short visit, aimed at increasing her popularity. There had been failed attempts on her life and she was now accompanied at all times by two hairy, grim-faced bodyguards who stood six feet seven tall.

On the day of the visit Stevie's parents had to go to Fife to an orphanage, so Stevie, Bruce, and Fergal had gone on their own to see Queen Victoria and Prince Albert. Bruce had taken extra care with the linen cloth covering his wicker basket and had even put on a Stuart tartan scarf round his neck in support of the Queen.

Stevie and Fergal, on Christine Rump's instructions, wore two neatly pressed white shirts under their coats. Bruce wore a sleeveless knitted green pullover with a white shirt underneath it and his black trousers. But he had insisted on wearing an old green woollen checked cloak over it and a plumed hat, despite objections from Christine. His Aunt Lucy had made it for him. She was the last link of any family he had, apart from his distant cousin, Clovis. After he had said the cloak reminded him of his Aunt Lucy, Christine Rump guiltily felt very sad and said it was fine to wear it. She felt sorry for the little cat, because she knew how much he had loved his aunt. He had lost his parents at a young age and his aunt had been all he had in the way of family, apart from his cousin Clovis. But he never saw Clovis, just received the odd letter from him.

After Selena, the Queen of the Witches, had won the War of the Mermaids, Bruce's Aunt Lucy had been taken away by the witches to be a slave. Despite numerous searches for her she had never been found. Stevie, Fergal, and Max and Christine Rump believed her to be dead, and now never mentioned her in case it upset Bruce.

"Stevie, what do we call Queen Victoria?" asked Bruce.

"If we get to speak to her, you mean?" came Stevie's response.

"Your Majesty," replied Fergal. "You will also have to take a bow when you say it."

Bruce practised his bow. Being vertically challenged, with his dumpy body and short, striped legs, he was nearer to the ground than the others.

"I was going to wear my cap, but I think I will wear my plumed hat so I can take that off at the same time as I bow. I think it will make me look lordly," said Bruce, spinning round and taking a further bow.

"Hey, Bruce, I hate to burst your bubble of meeting Queen Victoria, but with all the crowds you might never get to see her."

"Stevie, man, we will get to meet her. I'm sure of it," said Bruce earnestly, swatting an unfortunate fly that happened to be flying in his direction with his paw. "Why, I've even heard she likes cats, so I'll get us to meet her. She will love me. How could she not? Not sure about you two, though."

Stevie and Fergal knew he was probably right, and laughed. Out of all of them, Bruce was the one she would warm to. Despite the reports of her sombreness, she was believed to like cats.

The day of Queen Victoria's visit seemed to approach quickly in the following weeks. Edinburgh High Street was ablaze with activity, and had been completely transformed. The whole street was now festooned with streamers and even the fisherwomen were lined up with the huge crowds, wearing freshly washed white caps and aprons and hoping to meet the monarch. The slimy, pea-soupy fog that seemed to hang gloomily in the air in the previous weeks had now lifted, and the normally smog-filled air smelt fresh and clean. The sound of pipers dressed in Stuart tartan kilts filled the air and plumed black-and-white horses in horse-drawn carriages trotted along the road, their necks covered in garlands of flowers.

Seated in the first carriage – an open-backed carriage – that came through the street was the Lord Provost, with his haughty-looking lady wife. A uniformed driver drove slowly so they could wave out of the carriage and they did this with great importance, as if it were them that the crowds had come to see. They soon lost their sense of importance when two rotten tomatoes hit the face of the Lord Provost's wife, to her horror, splattering her powdered wig with tomato pips.

The tomato assassin then ran off through the vast crowds, and no one was able to capture him. Little Jimmy McMorrow, a little brown street monkey, was a phenomenal runner and there was no chance of him ever being caught, racing as he did on all fours down the high street, pursued by a red-faced policeman blowing his whistle at him.

"Look … look … Wow, look at that," said Bruce, pointing ahead, jumping up, and almost bursting with excitement. "It's the carriage."

A highly polished black carriage covered in red and pink roses came into view.

"If we get to the castle quickly, we might get to the front," said Bruce, his tail twitching with excitement.

Stevie and Fergal looked at each other and shrugged.

"Come on quickly, guys," shouted Bruce, racing ahead. The little cat was determined to see the Queen. His mouth was pinched in grim concentration and his head was full of thoughts as he imagined what he would say to her.

Stevie and Fergal sighed and raced after him.

For an inactive little tabby cat, when he wants to do something he is an exceptionally fast walker, thought Stevie, breathlessly.

With a flapping of wings behind him, Fergal half-flew and half-ran in his wake. The cormorant struggled to keep up with them.

After racing up Princes Street and up to the castle, which led on to Castle Hill, they were ahead of the crowd now. In the distance they could see the hills of Arthur's Seat and Salisbury Crags.

Bruce beamed at Stevie and said,

"We've done it. We're at the front. She's bound to talk to us now."

As they looked across to the entrance of the castle Queen Victoria was led out of the carriage by the Lord Provost, who bowed and held on to her hand as she came down the carriage steps. The Queen was wearing a dress of Royal Tartan, with a loose blue shawl over her shoulders. On her head was a white starched bonnet, with an ostrich feather planted on the side of it. The Queen's hair had been parted on the middle, and small ringlets lay loosely under her hat. Large light blue eyes peered out of a pale face as she looked regally across at the excited crowd. Albert, the Prince Consort, followed down the steps after her, dressed in a high-collared black frock coat with high-waisted trousers, but he shivered at the cold wind that had appeared to wrap around him.

Bruce held on to his wicker basket tightly. He was sure she would love his trifle. The crowd, however, were now ecstatic, and a large hat landed on Bruce. He pushed it off his shoulder. The men in the crowd threw their hats further into the air, shouting heartily,

"Long live the Queen."

"Your Majesty!" shrieked Bruce, struggling to raise his voice above the chanting of the Scottish crowd. "Your Majesty," he shouted more loudly, jumping up and down to gain her attention. To his amazement, the Queen looked in his direction and made a movement as if she was coming towards him.

"Oh my God … She's coming. She's coming," squealed Bruce.

"Calm down, Bruce," said Stevie, trying to control the shaking cat, who was now a bundle of nerves. Bruce, Stevie, and Fergal walked towards the Queen, but Bruce was being pushed by the crowd. As he struggled with his basket someone lunged at him as they tried to get in front of him, and as they forced him forward he went flying into the air.

While he was struggling to hold on to his basket he slipped. The wicker basket flew above his head and the lumpy mass spilled out high into the air as the basket and the glass bowl came crashing to the ground on their way. The crowd were then showered with a mixture of cream, blackberries, and oatmeal. But an enormous portion of the trifle remained in the air, seeming to have a mind of its own, and a strong wind pushed its sticky matter further up high into the sky.

As Queen Victoria walked up, smiling towards Bruce, she seemed oblivious of the lump of flying trifle now dangerously about to land on her head. After racing over and grabbing her, Bruce pushed her to one side. Horrified, she tried to free her hands, but Bruce hung on firmly as he tried to move her away from the fruit that was now splattering the crowd.

"An assassin!" screamed someone from the crowd.

"It's only a trifle," shouted Bruce, as he let go of Queen Victoria's struggling hands. "It's a trifle," he repeated. But the crowd were venomous, and edged dangerously towards him.

"It's a rifle. He said he's got a rifle. He's going to kill our Queen. Let's get him. Grab the assassin," screeched a hairy-eared Scotsman who, being hard of hearing, had misheard what Bruce had said.

"Oh my God. This can't be happening. Let's get out of here, Bruce. They think you came here to kill the Queen." A shocked Stevie grabbed Bruce, who had now developed purr hiccups with the shock of it.

"Come on. Move," he ordered. He dragged a traumatised and struggling Bruce behind him. Fergal flapped his large wings to their full extent behind him, giving the pair time to escape. But he was shoved aside by a burly bodyguard. The man must have been at least six feet seven, and was dressed in a green tunic in Black Watch tartan with a stripe of deep crimson down the centre of it. He made gigantic strides towards Bruce and Stevie, but they raced ahead of him.

The bodyguard briefly glanced back at Fergal and snarled. To Fergal's horror, he saw the bodyguard change in a split second and have an almost inhuman look about him. His pupils had an unnatural colour about them, and reflected strangely in the light. Then he snarled and his mouth parted to show yellow, pointed teeth, with a line of drool hanging off his misshapen lips. It was a terrifying image. It was not a human face looking back at him.

But, as Fergal tried to get a further look, the man was gone. On looking around it seemed that nobody had seen what he had seen. As he shook his head, Fergal thought his eyes must have been playing tricks on him. Now, worrying about Bruce and Stevie, he flew high into the air above the mud-stained cobbled street to find them.

What they didn't know was that they were being followed.

Chapter 3

Two extremely embarrassing months later, Stevie, Fergal, Bruce, and Mr Beavis the solicitor were about to set off for the gruelling journey to Howly Island. Christine Rump, Stevie's mother, had had to sort their mess out. She had managed to get Bruce out of the Tower of London and explain what had really happened: that it had all been an unfortunate mistake, and that Bruce had been trying to present a home-made trifle to the Queen and not trying to assassinate her.

Stevie's parents then decided that the best thing was to let the matter die down and get the boys out of the way in case it escalated further. Howly Island seemed the only answer. His parents felt that Mr Beavis, being a solicitor, would be a very responsible adult and the three would be perfectly safe in his company. Little did they know the terrible danger the boys would be facing.

After climbing on to the gaily painted steam train run by the Glasgow and Edinburgh Company, Stevie, Bruce, and Fergal waved Christine and Max Rump goodbye, which was exciting and sad at the same time. There had been a near disaster when Bruce had jumped on to the iron step and, being so small, had nearly fallen under one of the train wheels. Fortunately, he had managed to grab the large shiny brass handle on the train carriage to steady himself.

The first-class emblazoned carriage, in a highly polished russet brown, was separated from the second and third class and it airily showed its importance.

"Come on, boys, no time for delays," spoke Mr Beavis in his best headmaster's voice.

Stevie, Fergal, and Bruce followed meekly behind him like naughty pupils with their cases. Bruce's case was nearly the same size as he was. He had insisted on taking far too much stuff.

The black steam train was incredible. Even people who were not travelling on it came to look at in amazement. A reporter had even written about it in the *Edinburgh Herald* as an object of beauty.

As the crowds waved to their loved ones, a tall, formidable-looking cheetah dressed in a long cream rubber raincoat with a brown fedora perched low on his head had been following the boys and Mr Beavis while they climbed on to the train. While furrowing his brow and narrowing his long, heavily lashed orange eyes, he proceeded to lick his pencil and write something in his small notebook. He sensed the boys would be trouble and frowned, deep in thought.

As the train pulled out he walked away. The cheetah had found out where the boys were going and would catch them up later. But first he would check out Christine and Max Rump and see if he could find out any further information on them.

Stevie, Bruce, and Fergal settled in the first-class roomy carriage with padded walls, red silk curtains, and plush, charcoal-grey seating piped with gold thread at the edges. Mr Beavis ushered them to place all the cases under their seats.

"My assistant, Cedric, will not be joining us, unfortunately, but I'm sure that will not be a problem," said Mr Beavis, a short, flushed-looking man with pale blue eyes. He wiped his spectacles and placed them on top of his well-rounded stomach as he spoke. He then wiped his permanently pink, sweating brow with the neatly folded brown-checked handkerchief that had been in his breast coat pocket. His bald head was like a shiny pink ball. Even his little round ears glistened. The small, thin lips on his face did not seem to match his eyes and nose. They appeared to be their own island, set at a downturned angle in a permanently disapproving expression.

"Mr Beavis, what happens when we get off at Glasgow Station?"

"We will walk to the riverbank and travel by a steamer on the River Clyde. This will go as far as Greenock. Then we will get a horse and carriage to Oban. From Oban we will have to get a boat to Howly Island," replied Mr Beavis, looking rather stern-faced at the boy. Stevie's confident manner was already annoying him. In his book, boys should be seen and not heard, and most certainly not ask questions.

"What time will we get to Howly Island?" asked Fergal.

He was met with a completely different response by Mr Beavis, owing to the fact that Fergal was his client.

"Sir, we should reach Howly Island by four o'clock, in time for tea," he said, smiling at Fergal. He noticed that the cormorant was wearing a rather expensively cut suit and was dressed in most suitable attire – unlike, he thought, the lanky, fair-haired scruffy boy and the filthy-looking, mangy tabby cat that were travelling with him. "You will have more papers to sign, I am afraid, but once that is done Loch House will be yours, to do with what you wish. I will take you to see the tenants in your properties. The leases will need to be altered in your name. But we can do all this for you, Fergal."

"Fergal, you're going to be a landlord," said Bruce. "Wow … Imagine. You will own houses and have tenants. How cool is that?"

Mr Beavis sniffed and raised an eyebrow at Bruce as the cat spoke, and then moved slightly further back into his leather train seat as if Bruce had some unpleasant disease he did not wish to catch.

Fergal beamed back at Bruce.

"I know. I can hardly believe it."

"What have you brought us for lunch, Bruce?" asked Stevie, cutting into the conversation, as he was now starting to feel hungry.

"Home-made pork pie, the last of my lattice apple pie, sardine sandwiches for me, and my triple-layered cheese scones," the tabby cat said, as he smiled back. Then he stopped speaking, as he thought he might have some breakfast food stuck between his teeth. So he rifled through his right coat pocket and produced from it a gnarled rat's foot, which he then proceeded to use as a toothpick.

"Oh, that is gross. Put that away. I thought my mum told you to throw it out," said Stevie, feeling the need to puke as he stared in hypnotic horror at the grimy grey object.

"Well, she thinks I did," said Bruce, guiltily, now intent on sucking the grime out of one of the pads of his paws.

"Put it away and stop doing that," shouted Fergal, while glaring at Bruce, embarrassed that Bruce had shown them up in front of the solicitor.

"Aw, man … Oh, all right," sighed Bruce as he scrunched his face up and gave up with his grooming. He was annoyed and did not understand why they were making such a fuss. He then placed the dried-up grey rat's foot back in his sticky trouser pocket.

Watching him was Mr Beavis, who stared at him and pursed his lips in displeasure to blot out the revolting image. Then took out his neatly folded copy of *The Times* from his briefcase, shook it, laid it in line with the cat's face to wipe out the image, and shook his head to himself in disgust..

Disappointingly, the train journey to Glasgow became extremely unpleasant. The carriage kept rocking from side to side as the train passed hills clad with rural villages, and at one point Stevie half-fell asleep then woke up, thinking he had been riding on a horse.

The train went at fifteen miles per hour, a speed sensation in 1842. This was all explained by Mr Beavis, who went on to mention that four passenger trains ran a day, with only two on Sundays, and that it was lucky they were in first class as there was less vibration on the suspension wheels.

But his train talk started to get boring. Fergal soon fell fast asleep and Bruce, as soon as he had closed his eyes, suddenly started snoring loudly. The only person now awake and listening to Mr Beavis was Stevie, but a kick on the ankle from Stevie soon woke Bruce up. He half-opened his eyes, yawned, and pulled a face to himself. Then he looked out of the window. The rattling train, leaving trails of billowing smoke in its wake, had started to pass bucolic country villages, fields of corn, and plough horses.

It – at last – came to a stop at a remote railway station as people came on board. Bruce watched a black cat dressed in a nun's habit struggled to climb on to the step with six excited ginger kittens, four of them dressed in blue and white sailor suits, and two female kittens wearing well-starched pinafore dresses. A smiling Bruce watched as eventually the nun managed to coax the last one, who was very nervous, to step on board the train. The train then moved on, passing a dense black forest, which made the carriage seem quite dark.

It was then that something happened that made Bruce's smile drop. Something came out of the forest, and he watched in an unbelieving, stunned silence.

It was a black figure. The image became clearer and his large cat eyes now saw a hunched, lumbering shape. It was moving and was quite close to the train now. Bruce continued to stare. At last he could see it quite clearly. It seemed like a huge animal wearing a green tunic and standing on its hind legs.

"Look at that," he shouted. "Over there ... Look ... look." He pointed with his paw in the creature's direction. But Fergal was still fast asleep, his beak snapping open and shut, with his eyes tightly shut as if he were dreaming, and Stevie was listening with interest to Mr Beavis's talk about steam trains.

Outside the window the creature seemed to hear him shout, and turned and looked towards the train. It stared intently at Bruce and bared its teeth. Blood dripped from its chin as it stared arrogantly back at him. It looked at first like a monstrous black wolf, but then he saw it was only half-wolf. The other part of it seemed human.

"Oh, Jeez ... Oh, Jeez," said Bruce, as he jumped up in his chair in fright. As he said this the train started to speed up.

"What's wrong, Bruce?" asked Stevie, breaking out of his conversation with Mr Beavis and finally turning around.

"Over there. Horrible ... horrible. A huge wolfy thing dripping blood. Look. Look, man, look."

But, as Stevie turned to look, the train had passed on to the next village.

"I saw a creature. Its face was covered in blood. It was a big wolf walking on its hind legs, and it was dressed in a green tunic. But it was much larger than a wolf, almost like some huge great big monster."

"You were asleep, Bruce. You must have dreamt it."

"I did not, Stevie. I tell you, it was a wolf. I saw it." But despite his rants no one would believe him. They thought he had dreamt it. Eventually he gave up and folded his paws across his chest in a sulk.

"Come on, get out your food basket, Bruce," said Stevie, as he tried to appease him.

And, with the word 'food' mentioned, Bruce really did brighten up.

"It's in my trunk. Can you get it out for me?" asked Bruce, food taking over. He was now not bothered whether they believed he saw a monster or not.

Stevie didn't need asking twice, and pulled the trunk from under his seat. The food had been placed in a wicker basket covered in thin blankets. There was more food than clothes in the trunk.

"No wonder your case was so heavy," laughed Stevie.

"There're apples in my red jumper sleeves as well, if you guys want one," replied Bruce, intent on carefully removing dishes from the basket.

The smell of baked food woke Fergal up, and everyone's mouth began watering as Bruce removed thick brown paper and string. A huge square pork pie with a pattern of paw prints round the pastry edges appeared before their eyes. Its golden, honey-coloured pastry glimmered in the dim light, and a smell of baking now filled the air. Even Mr Beavis looked impressed.

"You made this?"

"Yeah, it's my Cheshire pork pie recipe. There's a layer of apples in it and I spiced it with nutmeg, salt, and pepper," replied Bruce, going red with modesty.

"It looks very tasty," the solicitor responded hungrily, licking his dry lips and changing his tone towards Bruce.

"I'll cut you a piece, man," came Bruce's reply, as he sliced a chunk with his penknife from his jumper pocket. He placed it on some folded brown paper, which he used as a plate, and passed it to the solicitor.

When Mr Beavis tucked into the pie his face beamed with delight.

"This is superb. Why, the pastry is light as a feather."

"Bruce and Fergal used to be chefs on board ships," said Stevie, proud of his pals, as it was obvious that Mr Beavis was in heaven as he tucked into each delicious mouthful.

"Well, I'm more of a fine cuisine cook than he is," said Fergal snootily, getting jealous. "Bruce is more into home-cooked stuff."

"They are both really good cooks. People used to go wild about their food in the Caribbean," answered Stevie, revelling in their talent.

Bruce, Stevie, Fergal, and Mr Beavis tucked into the food happily. Fergal completely forgot about having to behave like a gentleman in in front of Mr Beavis and, after putting his feathery head back, he tossed bits of apple pie into the back of his large, open beak. The round apple lattice cake with its scalloped edges smelt heavenly as the aroma of cinnamon, nutmeg, and cloves wafted pleasantly into their nostrils.

Everyone was now full up and they were finishing off by eating apples, apart from Bruce, who had finished off his meal and was tucking into his squashed sardine sandwiches. With the food gone – well, apart from some telltale crumbs scattered on the train floor – they drank from bottles of water.

Their tummies pleasantly full, the group started, one by one, to fall asleep as the train trundled past Linlithgow Station – apart from Bruce, who had started thinking about the wolf he had seen at Ratho Station. The image had seemed so clear. But no one had believed him. It had looked straight into his eyes and bared its fangs at him. It had terrified him.

Were there monster wolves in Scotland? the tabby cat wondered, deep in thought as he scrunched his turned-up mouth. Then he shook his furry, striped head as if to wipe out the bad memory. He tried to go to sleep but could not. Instead he began watching Mr Beavis's newspaper slowly fall to the ground as his head moved further towards his chin and he began to gently snore, with a thin whistle following each snore in bursts. Just as he himself was about to finally fall into a deep sleep Stevie, who was now awake, shouted,

"We're nearly there. Look, that must be Glasgow." Stevie was standing up and pointing at the train window.

"Come, get the cases, boys," Mr Beavis said, yawning and brushing loose crumbs off his clothes.

Stevie and Fergal dragged the cases out one by one with Fergal helping, and they passed a calfskin case to Mr Beavis.

The platform at Glasgow smelt of smoke and was crowded and smelly. People jostled against them as they struggled to get to the entrance of the station, and the stench of body odour was strong in the crowd.

"Watch out for pickpockets, boys," whispered Mr Beavis, looking suspiciously as people passed him. His right hand stayed in his right suit pocket and he held firmly on to his wallet.

Bruce had the most difficulty because he was so small and was trying to carry his case, which was bulky, at the same time.

"You take mine. It will be easier for you to carry," said Stevie, seeing his friend struggling. Relieved, Bruce took the smaller case.

As they walked to the embankment, the group saw the paddle steamer come into view along the River Clyde. After paying for their tickets, they climbed aboard. A one-eyed boatman who smelt of tobacco grimaced at them as he placed snuff up each nostril.

"Nice warm welcome, I must say," said Fergal in a now even more pretend posh voice.

"Shush. He'll hear you," whispered Stevie.

"Oh, look at my suit," moaned Fergal. "It's all creased."

Irritated, Stevie rolled his eyes and ignored him.

A group of people came on to the paddle steamer.

"Brrr ... it's getting cold," said Bruce as he pulled his knitted red wool jumper down over the top of his tail and placed his paws deep up into the sleeves. He was shivering. His short black trousers were quite a thin material. It was going to be a frosty journey to Greenock.

The paddle steamer set sail and gave a lurch as it reluctantly moved forward against the grey waters. A strong head of wind quickly pushed it further along across the rough, curving sea. As they passed sleepy lochs, castle ruins, and bleak hills, the sky became darker. The paddle steamer swayed from side to side as it worked hard to make the wind-defying paddles work, but only resulted in making Fergal feel quite sick.

After taking a bottle of water out of his pocket he sipped at it, hoping he wasn't going to vomit in front of Mr Beavis. Mr Beavis, however, had nodded off and would never have noticed, even if he had. The solicitor's round face was now bright red with the cold weather, and his mouth was wide open as he let out occasional snorts. A trail of spit dribbled down his mouth on to his tweed suit and then on to his brown silk waistcoat. This made Fergal look away quickly.

27

Chapter 4

Finally they reached the bay of Greenock. Stevie woke Mr Beavis as they collected their cases and they all climbed off the steamer. But there was no horse and carriage waiting for them there. Not even a fishing boat was in sight.

"Where are the horses and the carriage?" Mr Beavis demanded of the one-eyed man.

"Och, you'll be looking at least an hour. Aye, at least an hour it'll be," he repeated, irritated by the Englishman's accent.

"An hour ... Oh, what a pain," said Stevie.

"I'll freeze to death if it gets any colder. I'm sure I'm getting icicles on my beak," Fergal moaned. "This suit isn't that warm," he added, shivering as a stray feather blew off his tail.

"This is ridiculous. We have to wait an hour for a carriage to take us to Oban?" Mr Beavis retorted, angrily scratching his forehead, perplexed.

The man replied, with a hint of amusement in his voice,

"Aye, an hour. Might be more. Depends on the weather." As he spoke, he engulfed Mr Beavis with his strong tobacco breath, which made him give an involuntary shudder.

"Is there anywhere we can go to get a drink?"

"Aye. You can walk down the hill. It'll get you to the shops. There's an inn called the Angry Dragon. The horse and carriages wait outside there, and you can get yourself a dram while you wait. That should stop your complaining."

The one-eyed man smirked. Then he looked Mr Beavis up and down, coughed, pulled his dirty-brown cap down over his face, and went back to his ropes on the boat, dismissing the strange group and muttering something under his breath.

"What a charming man. Come on, boys," said an irritated Mr Beavis.

The boys followed behind him. Stevie was struggling with Bruce's case. Walking down the long, curved path to the inn took less than ten minutes. Along the way they met a brown and white young bulldog dressed in a thick cotton mustard-coloured smock. Perched on his head was a brown felt hat and on his feet were thick black boots. He was shovelling extremely ripe manure into a cart on a farm, which gave off a nose-clenching pong. But when Stevie said a friendly hello the dog chewed its bottom lip, pulled a face at him, and then ignored him and carried on working.

"Friendly people and animals round here," whispered Fergal.

"I hope they're not all like that," replied Stevie, glumly.

"Well, at least having a drink at the Angry Dragon will kill an hour," said Stevie to Mr Beavis. The solicitor said nothing, just gave him a look of irritation. As well as Stevie's casual attire, the boy's fair, floppy hair and clothes were also things that annoyed him. Stevie was wearing a long black coat, his school trousers, and a grey wool jumper with heavy boots. The boots were scuffed and needed a polish, and Bruce's fawn cat hairs were all over the coat from when the cat had sat on it on the train.

There was a line of stone-built shops facing them as they walked up past a cobbler's. The Angry Dragon was a dingy grey building, and there was a commotion as they came up to it. A large brown eagle who looked quite moth-eaten was arguing with what seemed to be a warthog dressed in a grubby white shirt and short grey trousers. The eagle kept falling over and hurling more bird abuse each time, just as the warthog was about to walk away. The bird had had too much to drink and was swaying, and his long, pointed wings were half-opening and shutting as he struggled to stay upright. Finally the bird turned around and attempted to fly off, but ended up half-walking and half-flying down the road. The warthog scrunched up its face. Then it too walked away, but in the opposite direction.

Fergal and Bruce smiled at each other and stifled their laughter in front of Mr Beavis. Their smiles were quickly wiped off their faces when they saw the look on Mr Beavis's face. Mr Beavis tutted and pushed forward the heavy oak inn door, and they went inside.

A barmaid, a large pink pig in a high-necked beige dress with a white frilly apron, was washing glasses behind the bar.

"Hello. Settle yourself down, boys, and I'll come and see ta ya," she shouted across at them, speaking with a Scottish lilt. She had a large, round face, a snout nose and dimpled cheeks. Her frizzy strawberry-blonde hair fell in tired ringlets under a well-washed white cap. A plump animal, her pot belly strained under the large white apron and the dress she wore that covered it.

The group selected a long wooden table with a painting of a grey whale on the wall near the dusty fireplace. Alongside it was a Gothic-looking picture of an enormous black cat, with one of its paws holding a small boat in a rain-drenched swirling mass of waves.

"Look at that picture. It doesn't half give me the willies," remarked Bruce on noticing the black cat's face (which had been painted to look evil) with its mouth open, fangs displayed, as it held the boat filled with terrified-looking people in one of its heavily clawed paws as if it were about to eat them.

"That will be the notorious Black Cat of Bute," replied Mr Beavis as he stood up to have a good look at it.

"The Black Cat of Bute?"

"Oh, an old wives' tale, of course. A devil cat believed to bring ships down in this area."

"Ugh … Horrible picture. I may be a cat … but, man, I wouldn't want that on my wall, and I hope I never meet that cat."

"Yeah, me neither. I wonder if it's a true story," replied Stevie.

But no one answered. They were all intent on making themselves comfortable.

A burning log and coals gleamed from the welcoming, roaring fire as the strong smell of coal dust engulfed the room. Bruce, while trying to get as close as he could to the roaring fire, moved his back dangerously close to it and lifted his tail so his bottom could get warm. This resulted in it getting half-singed, but it didn't seem to bother him.

"What can I get ya, boys?" asked the sleepy-looking barmaid, looking directly at Mr Beavis as she came over to them.

"Could I have a large malt whisky, and whatever the boys are having?" beamed the solicitor as he produced change from a thick round leather wallet that looked handmade.

"I'll have a glass of your finest house wine," said Fergal, speaking with his heavily increased posh accent.

"No, you won't, laddie. Ya are too young. It'll be a soft drink or nothing," the barmaid replied, causing the cormorant to blush all the way to tip of his boots.

"Oh … eh … eh … Can I have lemon cordial then, please?" he spluttered.

"Can I have one as well?" said Stevie.

She nodded just as Bruce turned to her, so she got the full glare of his vivid green eyes as he asked sweetly,

"Could I have a glass of milk, if it's not a bother, ma'am?" As he spoke he lifted his eyebrow whiskers endearingly and purred softly.

Totally lost in his huge green eyes and Caribbean accent, she said,

"Certainly. Ah, what a lovely pussycat ya are." She stroked his head as she said it and then walked away.

Fergal pulled a face and said,

"Pass me the sick bucket, will you?"

"I think she likes me," responded Bruce, beaming happily.

"Where are ya going ta?" the barmaid asked Mr Beavis when she returned with the drinks laid on a little wooden tray.

"Oban, and then Howly Island. Can I ask you … Will a horse and carriage be coming shortly? We just need to get to Oban to get the ferry to the island as soon as possible."

"Howly Island … Oh, my word. Dinna go there. No one goes there. It's an evil place. Full of monsters. Horrible, horrible things happen there. I'm warning ya … Ya canna go there. There's a carriage coming soon. Go somewhere else than Howly Island." The pig shuddered as she spoke, as if trying to wipe out a memory too horrible to mention, and didn't reply to his question about the horse and carriage.

"Monsters?" said Stevie.

"Och, yes. No locals would dare to go back there now. They say the monsters drag people they catch into the Howling Forest and that is the last anyone hears of them."

"Utter nonsense, Mona," came a deep voice at the other side of the room, which sounded so loud it seemed to make the floor beneath her quake. "Stop frightening these poor people. Howly Island is perfectly safe. I have been there quite often and have never seen any of these so-called monsters."

The barmaid, seeing the woman talking, stopped speaking, lowered her eyes, and returned to the bar.

The woman speaking was milk-white, tall and thin, and at least six feet in height with small round dark eyes, which looked like overcooked currants. A long, thin nose hung hook-like over her narrow, crooked pale lips. Her lacklustre thin hair, which was quite strange, with coarse black sections arranged in a huge bun, looked like it had been glued together. Ramrod-straight, she was wearing a long, heavy black wool dress with a slight bustle. Over her coat hanger shoulders she wore a heavy bearskin cloak, and her long and bony white fingers were covered in sparkling rings. She walked swiftly across to the group, her dress rustling as she walked, and ushered someone behind her to come with her.

"Hello. My name is Myra Bloodvein. I couldn't help but hear what Mona was saying to you. I hope you do not think I was being rude, listening to the conversation." She was well-spoken and had an English accent. Myra then smiled, displaying slightly crooked, extremely large teeth.

"Oh, of course not," replied Mr Beavis, giving her his best smile.

"This is my daughter, Fenella. We are waiting for my sister, but she has not yet arrived." The strange woman pushed forwarded a pretty, sulky-looking fair-haired girl. She was dressed in a bright pink dress with a pink tartan cape covering her shoulders, which were rounded by puppy fat. Her hair was golden, and hung in tight, powdered curls around her face. But the large, long-lashed grey eyes had a vacant look about them. She stared at Bruce and said,

"Can I have that?" She poked a horrified Bruce in his tummy as she spoke.

"Of course, you can, Fenella. How much can I buy the little fat cat for?" Myra asked Mr Beavis brusquely.

"Umm, no, he is not for sale. He belongs to this group," replied an embarrassed Mr Beavis.

"What … for sale? Me – what you talking about? You joking me?" butted in a confused Bruce. His cheeks burnt up with embarrassment as he realised she was now being deadly serious.

Ignoring him, Myra said to Mr Beavis,

"Oh, all cats and birds are for sale, and I will give a good price for it. My daughter likes little furry animals like that. She keeps them as toys."

"Bruce is not for sale," replied Stevie, now stepping into the conversation. He was trying to control his temper and getting as angry as Bruce.

"Oh, I am sure any animal has a price. Wouldn't you agree, sir?" said Myra, ignoring Stevie, whom she regarded as just a child, and speaking only to Mr Beavis.

"Uh, well, yes, but unfortunately he is not mine to sell. He is a free animal."

"Yeah, that's right. I am a free animal and I am not for sale. Got it?" said Bruce furiously. His nervous hiccups now came back as he spoke, and the fur on his back was standing on end in thick spikes.

Myra tutted and gave Bruce an irritated look, but did not reply to him. Then she appeared to give up trying to buy Bruce and sighed, and asked pleasantly of Mr Beavis instead,

"Why are you all going to Howly Island?"

"I have inherited my Uncle McFetrich's estate," Fergal butted in, feeling left out of the conversation.

"You? A bird! A bird has inherited Remus McFetrich's estate?" said Myra, almost shouting back at him in disbelief.

"Well, yes. My solicitor and I are going to tie a few things up and I am going to see my tenants, as a matter of fact. I will be a laird, so I have a responsibility to check the estate and land." Fergal's accent appeared to be getting more upper-class with each sentence he spoke.

"But your uncle was human?" came Myra's rude reply.

"Yes, that's right, but my mother adopted me. Then she died. I have been away at sea for a few years. I only found out about my uncle when a solicitor contacted me in Edinburgh. My uncle had never married and he left everything to my mother in his will, which, on her death, was then passed on to me."

"I see," replied Myra icily. "Well, a cormorant inheriting Howly Island … That will be most unusual. I am sure the locals will be very pleased to hear about that." The cold look in her eyes made Fergal's glassy eyes blink nervously, and he decided she was horrible and that he didn't like her at all.

"If I can't have the cat can I have that ugly bird?" asked Fenella, butting in and pulling at Myra's dress hem to gain her attention.

"No, I am afraid you can't, Fenella. He also appears to be a free animal." She almost spat out the words as she spoke.

Fergal, listening in horror, flapped his wings in shock, which resulted in causing three of his small tail feathers to float out high into the air. The cormorant looked across at Bruce, who rolled his eyes at him and shook his head in sympathy with him.

"Oh, dear. What a pain. Looks like you are not for sale either," replied Bruce, ignoring Myra's penetrating gaze. Bruce, still furious, then stood up from the table and went across to the window to try and get away from her. "Hey, guys, there's a horse and carriage outside. Look."

"It must have come early. You're in luck," said the barmaid, who was now washing glasses. "If you get your cases, I'll let him know you're here. He's my uncle." The pig put down the damp cloth and the glass she had been holding and went outside to speak to a grey-haired old man dressed in a thick brown wool coat with a mushroom-coloured scarf wrapped around his neck.

The group struggled with their cases as they were getting up.

Mr Beavis quickly finished off his malt whisky then turned to Myra and her daughter, saying,

"Goodbye, ladies. If you ever need a solicitor, pray do take my card." He bowed to them and handed Myra a pristine white business card as he was about to make his way to the door.

"Thank you. It will, I assure you, be of interest to me. I am sure we shall see each other again. I expect very soon indeed," came Myra's strange reply.

"Let's hope never," muttered Fergal. "How rude was she?" he whispered to Stevie. "As if I would be for sale. Me? Huh. The cheek of it." Fergal twisted his beak to one side at the outrage of it and then began clucking to himself.

"Come on, let's get out of here," came Stevie's reply as he dragged Bruce along with him. Bruce was now giving Myra Bloodvein his famous stink eye. It wasn't often he disliked someone, but if he did he would look sideways at them, narrowing his eyes, and making the hair on his back stand on end to look threatening.

As they came outside the barmaid looked worried. Her forehead was furrowed as she saw them and went outside with them.

"Stay at Oban. Dinna go to Howly Island, lads."

"We have to go," replied Stevie.

"Please dinna go. It's a bad place, make no mistake. If I canna change your minds, all I will say is ... If you have to go, just take care." The sad-looking pink pig patted Bruce's soft furry head again as she spoke, much to his delight, and he gave a gentle purr in return. Even saying the words 'Howly Island' filled her with dread and she could not bear the thought of any harm coming to them, especially the chubby little cat in his oversized jumper.

As they looked across at Mr Beavis they realised that he had started discussing payment with the carriage driver, so he hadn't heard what the barmaid had been saying. The carriage driver waiting for them had a rather bored-looking piebald horse, who was called Duncan. The horse waited impatiently, while grinding one of his hooves into the ground and shaking his mane.

After walking over, Stevie patted the horse's head. The horse lowered his head as he stroked it, but then gave a sigh. While staring at the ground forlornly, he ground one of his hooves back into the ground in frustration. The horse hated doing this route. Strange things were beginning to happen on that island and it was a place he did not want to go anywhere near. The horse would have preferred to be playing in his field with his friend Brian, a donkey. After sighing once again, he lowered his head further down and continued to stare at the ground in self-pity.

Stevie, curious of what the barmaid had been saying inside the public house, asked her,

"Do you know Myra?"

"Myra Bloodvein? Oh, aye. Wish I didna know her. She's a nasty piece of work, a horrible witch. I would say keep ya distance from her. So different from her nice wee sister, Clarinda." As she said this, as if by magic, Myra appeared at the window and looked directly into the barmaid's frightened eyes.

"Why are you so scared?" asked Stevie, concerned.

"I have ta go," came the hurried reply. The pig gulped and began to tremble as she said this and went inside the inn, her tiny high heels clicking behind her as she lifted up her dress and walked inside.

"Did you see how scared she was of Myra?" Stevie looked at the door of the inn as he spoke to Mr Beavis.

"Oh, it will be nothing. She has probably been told off for giving out the wrong refreshments and is sulking," said Mr Beavis, unconcerned, and wiping his shining brow once again as a line of sweat trickled down it. "Come, everyone into the carriage. I have paid the driver."

With their cases loaded on top of the carriage and tied down with rope, the driver climbed back on to his seat. Fergal, Stevie, Bruce, and Mr Beavis made themselves comfortable on the leather seats. The driver then began making clicking noises to his horse.

"Come on, Duncan, laddie."

The horse snorted and shook his head, and the huge wheels of the carriage turned and began to move at a steady pace. The carriage passed through rolling green countryside, pastures and woodlands, and went past an old abandoned weaver's cottage. The weather then appeared to change for the worse and they welcomed the two brown tartan throws lying on the ground of the carriage, which they folded and placed over their knees. The carriage began to wobble, and twice Stevie had to hold on to Bruce to stop him falling off his seat.

"I'm starting to feel a bit sick," groaned Bruce, holding his striped tummy.

"We should be there soon, laddie," shouted the coachman. "Hold on there. It's not much longer."

Bruce really wished he hadn't eaten those sardine sandwiches on the train. He swallowed again and again as if to wipe out the memory. Having the milk hadn't helped either. To take his mind off it he peered out of the window.

"We will come to Oban soon," said Mr Beavis. "You will be able to get some fresh air, and we will then get the ferry across to Howly Island."

"Ugh … I just hope we get out of this carriage soon," groaned Bruce, still holding his tummy. Mr Beavis glanced across at the cat. He was now getting worried and thinking that he would have to talk

36

to the animal to get his mind off his travel sickness. The thought of cat vomit in the carriage was not something he relished.

"Look behind us, over there. What's that?" pointed Stevie as he looked out of the window.

"It's like a long line of black clouds," replied Mr Beavis, screwing his eyes up as he looked out of the window and up to the sky. The blackness seemed to come nearer to them. "No, I appear to be wrong. It looks like a flock of birds." Mr Beavis screwed up his eyes further as he spoke.

"It's not birds," shouted the terrified carriage driver. "Everyone get down. Cover yourself in blankets."

"What on earth?" began Mr Beavis.

"It's vampire bats. Cover yourselves. I'm going ta have ta speed up. Come on, Duncan. Go, boy, go."

The horse needed no encouragement. He had been bitten before. The carriage rocked from side to side as the horse and carriage raced down winding country lanes followed by what looked like a black squall coming after them.

"Did he say vampire bats?" whispered Bruce, now half-hidden under one of the blankets.

White-faced, Stevie nodded back in reply.

"Oh, man. Don't vampires drink blood?" wailed a terrified Bruce.

"They're not real vampires, Bruce. They're bats," replied Stevie, trying to calm him down.

"But they could be vampires. Oh no. What if they get us and drink our blood and they turn me into a vampire cat? Oh my God. Jeez ... I don't want to turn into a vampire cat." The little cat shook with fear and burrowed deeper into the blanket, so all that could now be seen was his huge, staring eyes peeping out.

"It's all right, Bruce. The carriage driver knows what he's doing. We'll be all right." But Stevie's voice did not sound convincing.

The carriage raced along dusty roads, shaking violently across the narrow wooden bridge, and still it went on at a heart-wrenching pace. Duncan was an exceptionally fast horse, but it was the fear of getting bitten that spurred him on.

"Come on, Duncan. Faster," screamed the carriage driver. "Faster. Go faster, boy."

The horse charged along at full speed, leaving a cloud of dust in his wake and frantically trying to escape the black cloud of bats in the distance.

The nail-biting journey seemed to last forever until Fergal said,

"Hey, look, they are disappearing."

As they looked out of the back window the group could see a black line go up into the sky and slowly start to fade.

"They've given up on us," shouted the breathless carriage driver.

"What on earth are these creatures?" asked Mr Beavis. He had now regained his composure and found, to his horror, that he had been holding hands with Bruce.

"They are vampire bats from the howling wood. Evil little creatures with long black wings. They swoop down on ya and on animals, looking to drink ya blood. I usually take my shotgun, but forgot to bring it this time. That usually does the trick."

Mr Beavis after wrenching his hand away from a clinging Bruce, replied,

"What type of place have we come to?"

"Och … It was not always like this, but something has happened to the place. The vampire bats never used to come out of the forest. Folks are leaving here."

"What do you think is happening here?" asked Mr Beavis.

"I think that pure evil has come ta Greenock, that's what I think," replied the carriage driver fearfully, but he wouldn't be drawn on the subject further, saying instead, "We will have ta stop. Poor Duncan will need some water or he won't be able ta go on. Poor lad has exhausted himself. You can get oot of the carriage if ya want while he drinks his water. It will be the only stop now."

"Are you sure it's safe to get out?" asked Mr Beavis.

"Och, yes. The bats will have given up and will now be lying in wait for some other poor beggars."

Everyone climbed out of the carriage. Bruce handed a glass bottle of water around for everyone to drink. They all drank from it apart from Mr Beavis, who had his own silver drink bottle. It was beautiful countryside, but all that could be heard was Duncan slurping noisily from his bowl of water. Stevie went up and patted him on the head as he drank.

"Good boy, Duncan," he said kindly to the exhausted, sweating horse.

He looked up with water-filled nostrils and then continued drinking the water noisily.

"Look," shouted Fergal to Stevie. As he got up to stretch his legs he had noticed something fluttering on the back of the carriage, but it was only the wind making it move. It was a dead bat. It hung on the side of the carriage, its eyes closed. The creature was ink-black with a furry muzzle, but its wide mouth was open and two enormous fangs hung out of the front.

Stevie gulped, raised his eyebrows, and said,

"I'm sure glad that didn't land on me."

The carriage driver, looking at the bat, removed it from the carriage and threw it away.

"Come on, everyone, get back in the carriage," said Mr Beavis.

"Say did you see those fangs, Stevie?"

"I did, Bruce. Frightened the living daylights out of me. Can you imagine it if they had caught up with us?"

"I don't want to think about that. C'mon, let's get back in the carriage, hey, man. They might decide to come back and get us," came Bruce's almost squeaky reply.

Chapter 5

The rest of the journey to Oban was uneventful but everyone was ill at ease, as if waiting for something to happen to them. Bruce tried to cheer everyone up, and mentioned Cousin Clovis. Mr Beavis, hearing Bruce speaking about his clever cousin, Clovis, and once again mentioning a bizarre flying contraption his cousin was building, finally sighed and closed his eyes and pretended to go to sleep.

Fifteen minutes later the horse and carriage groaned to a halt and the carriage driver shouted back to them,

"We're here, in Oban."

"Can you take us to McFarrell's bakery? I have to collect the keys to the house we are going to."

"Certainly, sir," came the driver's reply to Mr Beavis, but the horse was not happy and reared up. He just wanted to go home.

Oban was a fine-looking crescent-shaped place. They saw it was a large fishing port as the dusty carriage turned its large wheels, which almost groaned under the weight it carried. Facing Oban on a hill was a line of shops and, far in the distance, were some conical-shaped dark green hills.

They passed a fancy hat shop, Oban's distillery – which was an austere, prison-like building – some Victorian houses, and finally came to a bakery nestled at the end of the street. The bakery was painted in a chocolate brown, with shuttered windows. In its window it boasted an array of delicious-looking cakes, gingerbread, and loaves, which stared out in all their glory. The smell of cakes coming from the shop was divine.

The carriage stopped and Mr Beavis, who by now was standing on the small step, climbed out. Then came the smell of newly baked bread, strong in the air.

"Can I come with you?" asked Bruce, sniffing the air appreciatively and slightly purring.

"If you wish, but there's nothing to see. It's only a bakery," came Mr Beavis's preoccupied reply.

"Yes, but there might be something nice for us to eat."

"The housekeeper will most certainly have prepared a meal for us."

"I would, if I may, just like to look in the shop, Mr Beavis."

"As you wish," came Mr Beavis's irritated reply. He was very much a snob and did not really want to be seen with Bruce.

Bruce had not waited for a reply. He had already jumped down, and he went with the solicitor into the shop. As they opened the door a bell went off. A large, twenty-stone hessian sack of flour lay by the right side of the door. Bruce shut the door and nearly tripped over it.

The smell of home-made bread now filled the air. He beamed with pleasure and looked at the counter. A fine plate was facing him, with a long, oblong-shaped piece of shortbread with cherries placed in the centre of it and sprinkled with sugar. Beside this was an array of marzipan sweets and cakes, which were iced in almond paste. They were topped with royal icing, piped decorations, and topped off with fresh fruit. The aroma of sugared dough baking was thick in the air as a small figure came out from a door behind the counter.

"Can I help you gentlemen?" asked a short-haired black female cat, who spoke softly in a Scottish accent. She was dressed in a long wide red calico skirt, with a high-collared frilled white blouse that was finished off with a red spotty bow at her neck. Covering her skirt was a long white frilly apron. As she walked towards them Bruce could see she was wearing polished hobnail black leather boots, which clattered and had traces of flour on the toecaps.

Bruce stared into her emerald-green eyes. Her eyebrow whiskers were sticking out like antennae as she looked back at Bruce. He looked adoringly at her. Because she was not getting a response from Bruce, the black cat turned and asked Mr Beavis if she could help him.

"Eh, yes, we have come for the key to Loch House for the McFetrich estate. I am Mr Beavis, the solicitor handling the estate," replied the solicitor stiffly.

"Ah ... Mr Beavis ... Good heavens ... I was just thinking about you. I have been waiting for you. I'll just go and get it. Just wait here." The black cat smiled and went swiftly out of the room, her long black tail swaying behind her. Bruce's eyes followed her every step.

As the door closed behind her he looked around the bakery. A brown wooden seat was against one of the walls. Above it was a poster of a black-haired male opera singer, with a shock of dark hair and enormous black sideburns framing the sides of his face. The opera singer was wearing a white cloak and white trousers tucked in black boots. In large red letters the poster said these words: *The Great Elvo*. It was a singer Bruce had never heard of.

The black cat returned with the key and handed it to Mr Beavis.

"Thank you. Can I have your name, please, if you would be so kind? I just need to write a report."

"Aye, certainly. My name is Callie McFarrell." The black cat gave a deep-throated purr and her long white whiskers twitched as she spoke the words.

"Er, Miss, can I have five pieces of that cherry shortbread, please? And the large pound cake, please?" burst in Bruce, hiccupping slightly.

Callie McFarrell nodded and began placing the shortbread and the cake in large paper bags. But to do this she had to move a large white jug of frothy brewer's yeast, which lay dangerously close to the edge of the counter. Her long, curled nails were beautifully manicured, something Bruce thought odd for a baker.

"Gee, your baking is amazing, miss."

"Thank you, sir. We have kept all our family recipes, *and* we do try to bake new ones. Try a piece of my chocolate ginger loaf." The black cat handed two large golden slices on a sample plate painted with a green squirrel to Bruce, and then to Mr Beavis.

"Wow ... Oh, this is so good," murmured Bruce happily. He bit into it as the dark chocolate slowly melted into his mouth, and then a warm taste of ginger filled the whole of his mouth. He was in heaven.

"Yes, it is indeed. Well, thank you very much, miss. We will have to be going," came the hurried reply from Mr Beavis, who was anxious to get going while Bruce was paying for his items.

"Thank you," shouted Bruce, staring in a kittenish manner into Callie McFarrell's green eyes as he was reluctantly dragged by the solicitor away from the counter. He continued to stare back at Callie in fascination.

"Come on, Bruce. We have to go."

"Bye," said Bruce, smiling to her stupidly as he clutched at the cinnamon-smelling paper, but she did not appear to hear him as she bent down to drag a flour sack into another room. Mr Beavis, irritated, grabbed his arm, and the pair half-fell out of the shop. Bruce, still staring back, transfixed at the shop, was grabbed roughly once more by an extremely impatient Mr Beavis. Bruce followed behind him, bringing a baking aroma with him.

"They smell nice," came Stevie's voice as he looked at Bruce's packages.

"Oh, it's cherry shortbread, and I also bought a pound cake for us all. The baking in there, Fergal, is so good. You would love it," replied Bruce, as he placed the purchases carefully in his case.

"It seemed to me you were more interested in the lady baker," Mr Beavis responded disapprovingly.

"What's that?" said Fergal, giving a squawk. With mischief in his sparkling, light blue eyes he jumped on the sentence.

"It's nothing," burst in Bruce, going red with embarrassment.

"I think I might go in the shop," replied Fergal, sucking up his cheeks and making kissing noises at Bruce.

"No, you won't, Fergal. We have to get going," replied Bruce, desperately.

Fergal continued to make kissy noises until Stevie told him to shut up. The bird just chuckled and eventually stopped. He was now bored with tormenting a lovesick Bruce and was more interested in their surroundings.

"Driver, can you take us to the harbour, please?" asked Mr Beavis. His eyes were scanning the view ahead of him.

The driver nodded in reply and, once he had checked everyone was seated, made a clicking noise to Duncan and lifted the reins. The carriage went back downhill. It seemed very steep. In the distance they could see the tied fishing boats on the surface of the sea.

After stopping at the harbour everyone climbed out of the carriage. Mr Beavis thanked the driver and paid him. With their cases all unloaded, he looked around him. A large dark green wooden fishing boat was half-mounted on the shoreline. A golden Labrador dressed in a baggy, thick-ribbed navy fisherman's jumper was bringing a box of fish into the harbour and passing it to a pug dog. A black guillemot with a sooty black plumage had taken advantage of the situation by stealing a fish. It bashed it against a rock and flew off with its prize as it was shouted at by the angry pug dog.

"Would you be able to take us to Howly Island?" Mr Beavis asked the Labrador.

The dog looked up, his huge honey-brown eyes unblinking, and said in a broad Scots accent,

"You want ta go to Howly Island?"

"Yes, that's right."

"Not a nice place to be travelling ta, sir," the dog replied, frowning and pushing a dark brown cap further up his forehead.

"Well, it's business. Can you take us now?"

"Aye, sir. Just let me get the rest of my fish out ma boat."

The Labrador removed all the fish, and handed over another box of fish to his pug companion. Mr Beavis was not happy about having to climb into a boat smelling of fish, but time was moving on and he wanted to get to Loch House before dark. It was also getting quite cold, and he was shivering. The clothes he was travelling in were not warm enough.

"There are some blankets in the back of the boat if you get cold. The wind is coming up, so we are gonna have bad weather," said the Labrador on noticing this while looking up at the overcast skyline and frowning.

"No, I am sure we will be fine," replied the solicitor, trembling and giving a tired smile, but also not wanting to wrap himself in the fish-stained woollen blankets.

With all the fish boxes removed, everyone climbed into the boat and sat down, after struggling with their cases. The Labrador climbed in after them and cast off the rope. He placed himself at the bow of the boat and picked up the oars. Now seated, the dog raised the oars just above the water's surface and pushed them forward. The water of Oban was dark blue just off the Firth of Lorn. A spray of seawater hit the boat as it lurched forward, but then small waves of water began to gather up and batter the boat furiously as it went deeper into the sea.

"How long will it take to get to Howly Island?" asked Stevie, wiping droplets of seawater off his face.

"Less than an hour," came the oarsman's reply, his face scrunched up deep in concentration as he built up his rhythm with his oars.

The further the boat went into the water the more the water became darker, turning a black-grey. Curious basking seals on rocks came down and popped their heads above the water near them in mild curiosity as the boat went by. It was now ice-cold, and until then Bruce had been the only one using the blankets to keep warm. But then Stevie had given in and had now snuggled under them with him. Fergal and Mr Beavis, although cold, refused to go under the blankets because they were not willing to have their fine attire smelling of fish.

"You can tell we are coming ta Howly Island," said the Labrador, breaking the silence.

"How?"

"Look at the black water and sky. It's a bad place ta be travelling to, and no mistake."

The seawater had completely changed in colour, as if someone had poured an enormous pot of thick black ink into it.

"Why is it so bad?" asked Stevie.

"Och ... Full of bad people. They chased many of the locals away. I have heard there are monsters on that island. Long ago it was called Holy Island, but it's now called Howly Island. Huh ... more like Unholy Island. Not many of the locals live there now, apart from the poor wee minister John Aldridge after the minister Ballantyne left. He is a brave man, but I bet it'll not be long before he goes." The dog shook his head, as if imagining something horrible.

"I am sure a lot of this is hearsay. Your uncle would not have stayed on this island, Fergal, if it had been full of such evil people," said Mr Beavis, trying to make light of the conversation, but thinking to himself that coming to the island had been a very bad idea.

It then began to rain. Then came thunderstorms, and a zigzag flash of electrical red and orange lightning erupted over the distressed skyline. The group were pelted with bullets of rain as the fishing boat was pushed along by the strong current, and more seawater came into the boat. On the boat travelled, avoiding strange grey rocks sticking out of the water at curious angles. But they were not as odd as the prehistoric-looking caves that came into view – strange long thin black shapes. Even the sand looked black. A flock of crows filled the skyline. Then came a strange whistling wind in the distance.

As he shook his ears, Stevie asked,

"What's that?"

"It'll be the mermaids singing."

"Oh, we like mermaids. Will we get to see them?"

"Och ... You wouldn't like these ones from the Black Sea, laddie," replied the Labrador ominously. "They live in the deep Bonhomie's Caves in league with monsters, they say. Evil creatures: they have drowned many a poor fisherman round here."

"The mermaids are bad here?" replied Stevie, amazed.

"Oh, aye. Keep well away from them if you hear them singing ta you. Well, we're nearly there. I'll try and get as far doon ta the shoreline as I can. After that, ya are on your own. I never go any further than that."

"Oh, er, that's fine. Thank you. We'll get our cases together. My map has shown me it's not a long walk to Loch House ... unless we can get a carriage to take us there," replied Mr Beavis.

"Och ... I doubt you will get a carriage," replied the dog to a disappointed Mr Beavis. As he spoke, the boat came to the shoreline with an abrupt stop, making Bruce fall forward. Stevie had to catch hold of him to stop him from slipping. The Labrador helped everyone off with their cases and thanked Mr Beavis for his fare.

"Well, good luck ta you all," he said, looking concerned and scratching his chin. "Tek care of yourselves."

"Thank you," said Mr Beavis. "Can you tell me the direction we need to get to Loch House?"

"Aye. Follow the winding sand path up that hill. See there. It'll get ya on to the road. Walk along there. Ya will have a bit of a walk. There is a forest to the right. Dinna go in there. Many a traveller has lost their way in there. It's not a safe place ta go in. Make sure ta stay on the road."

"We all thank you for your help. Come on, let's get going." Mr Beavis turned to Fergal, Stevie, and Bruce, and said, "What a nuisance. It sounds like we will have a walk if we can't flag a carriage down."

The golden Labrador had now turned his back on them and moved his boat round, and all that could be seen was the green boat bobbing on the water as he went further back into the deep sea. A long, dark, and curling curious-looking shape from under the sea seemed to follow him as his boat went out of view from the beach. Stevie, Bruce, Fergal, and Mr Beavis were completely unaware of this strange curiosity, as they were facing away from the beach.

"Come on. Let's go up the path."

Mr Beavis led the way. Stevie took hold of Bruce's case and handed him the lighter one, and the group went up the twisting and winding black sand path. Tiny coals glistened the further they went.

"Oh, wouldn't you have thought there would be a carriage around here? My suit is filthy. Look at all this black dust," complained Fergal, and continued to complain, but no one responded to his moaning. They were just anxious to get to Loch House as quickly as possible. It had been a long day.

As they clambered up the path, minute black flies buzzed around them. Bruce swatted a few at a time. But then, after finding that walking and trying to catch flies with his paw was hard work, he gave up. The hill seemed to go on forever. Finally they reached the top, but a dirt road seemed to twist even further up.

"Oh ... Don't say we have another hill to go up," sighed Fergal. He was now getting hot and sweaty and flapping his wings to cool down, and half-flying and half-walking.

"According to this map, the house will be past the forest on the right," said Mr Beavis.

As they glanced across they saw thick black forest. Dried-out leaves blown by a shrill wind started to rustle as an owl hooted loudly, making Bruce jump.

"Man, that forest looks creepy, and look at the way those trees have been uprooted by the side of the road," said Bruce.

"Don't worry. We're not going through them. We'll only get lost. We've just got to stick to the path," replied Stevie, trying to reassure the nervous cat.

"Well, this is most unpleasant," Mr Beavis replied. "I did not expect to have to climb up a hill to get to the house." He wiped his permanently red forehead as he spoke. His handkerchief was now starting to look quite grey and grubby.

"Look at that … Look, there's a carriage." shouted Stevie excitedly.

As they looked ahead they saw it abandoned on the side of the road.

"It won't be much use without a horse," replied Mr Beavis sarcastically.

Stevie blushed with embarrassment, much to Mr Beavis's amusement.

"I wonder where the carriage driver and horse are."

"God knows," replied Fergal to Bruce. "Maybe one of the monsters dragged them away."

"Oh, shut up, Fergal," Bruce snapped. He was spooked already. His radar-like ears had picked up a strange sound with in the distance. He cocked his head to one side and said, "I can hear something. Listen. It sounds like a howl."

None of the others could hear anything.

"It sounded like a dog howling, or even a wolf."

"Bruce, why would wolves be in this place? We haven't even seen a sheep yet. Stop thinking about what you thought you saw on the train. You were just dreaming, and imagined it."

"I suppose you're right, Stevie. My ears must be bunged up. Oh, look at that … Nearly stood in it. Oh … look. Looks like dog poo." Bruce pointed at some slimy, dark poo disgustedly.

"Wouldn't get a cat doing something like that. Would you look at the strange colour? And it really stinks. Yuck. It will be some horrible smelly dog."

"Come along. We are not here to look at dog dirt. The housekeeper will be waiting for us," replied a thoroughly irritated Mr Beavis. Stevie, Bruce, and Fergal followed meekly behind him. After walking further they crossed over a rattling wooden bridge, which made their legs wobble.

In a large field was a herd of black-faced sheep. Bruce shouted to them, but didn't get a reply. They just looked blankly at him and moved further away from him. It seemed to be that these were animals that couldn't talk.

"Hey, man. It's like going back to the Dark Ages," said Bruce. "Imagine living in a place where animals can't talk."

"Some people would call that a blessing," said Mr Beavis drily, but Bruce didn't hear as he was still gazing at the sheep and hoping they would magically speak to him. But they didn't, and just looked vacant.

Chapter 6

The final hurdle up the hill was a struggle. No carriage driver had appeared, and the cases were now getting heavier. The group began pushing them in front of them half-heartedly. Stevie was using his big feet.

"Look in the distance. There it is. My map is bang up to date." Mr Beavis appeared to smile for the first time as he congratulated himself on how clever he was. He folded the map up carefully. After placing it back in his breast pocket, he said, "Well, Fergal, we should soon be coming to Loch House. In fact, the black speck in the distance … That could be it. The final point on the map is the castle ruins and then the McFetrich estate."

"I so hope so. I'm looking forward to a hot bath, a warm meal, and a change of clothing," came Fergal's grumpy reply. He was quite disappointed. He had expected to find a horse and carriage waiting for him to take him to the ancestral home. After all, he thought, wasn't he a bird of importance now?

Finally the group walked over a patchy pale green grassy verge. To the corner of it lay Loch House, surrounded by enormous oak trees and a greystone saddleback tower house, with what looked like thick medieval walls. A stagnant duck pond filled with parched leaves led up to six grass-covered steps and on to a large front door. A tied broom stood regimentally upright against the wall as if guarding the place.

A grimy brass bird's head knocker on the door faced the travellers. Mr Beavis lifted the beak of the bird door knocker. The noise was so loud that Fergal placed his hands over his ears.

"Wow … What a place," said Bruce in admiration, as he took in the size of the house. "Look, it even has a cottage on the right." On looking across, they could see a small white stonewashed cottage, which seemed to have been stuck on as an afterthought.

There was no answer to the knocking, so Mr Beavis impatiently knocked again on the door.

"Hey, look at the walls, Stevie. Jeez … Look at the cat scratches. They must be very large cats to have done that." Bruce touched the thick entrance wall and rang his paw across the thick, deep scratches. "I wouldn't like to meet them, that's for sure." His striped paw quivered as he continued speaking while still stroking the line of the scratches and placing his lips on it, trying to pick up a scent.

The sound of a chain being released and a bolt made him look up. As the door opened, a plump brown-eyed, grey-haired woman stared back at them, her dry, flat hair tied in a loose bun. She was wearing a long frilled white apron. Her thick waistline was hidden by her ample bosom and her swollen feet were encased in knitted brown slippers.

"Hello, madam. I am Mr Beavis of Beavis and McBeavis, Solicitors. You will have received my letter informing you of my arrival."

The woman nodded as Mr Beavis continued to speak.

"This is Fergal, who is due to take over his uncle's estate. I mentioned in my letter to you that he would be bringing his two friends, Stevie Rump and Bruce," said the solicitor with an air of importance, while pushing Fergal forward and looking behind him to show her Bruce and Stevie. He had found introducing Bruce difficult, as he didn't have a surname. This was something he found very strange.

"Pleased ta meet you, sirs," came the reply as the woman brushed a flour-covered tendril of hair off her right ear and gave a frown, adding another line to her forehead. "I am Kathleen Bucket. I am the housekeeper. We did wonder when you would show. I'll get Alwyn, my husband. He will bring your cases in and I'll make some tea. You must be parched from your travels."

She broke out of the sentence and turned to look behind her. She then shouted out in a shrill voice, having lost her posh accent,

"Alwyn … Come downstairs. The master's here."

A wild-looking, thickset man – ruddy-faced, with long stray white hairs coming out of his large fleshy ears and nostrils – appeared, wearing a hand-knitted brown jumper, a white shirt, and dark brown trousers. He was as wide as he was tall. He looked at them from under bushy black eyebrows and muttered, as if gritting his teeth,

"Hello. Pleased ta meet ya. Ah'll tek your cases." He picked up Bruce's, Mr Beavis's, and Fergal's cases with both hands and walked into the house.

"Did you see that? God, he must be strong. I can barely lift mine," said Stevie, who blew his cheeks out and struggled with his case as he walked inside the hall.

As they walked through the dark panelled-wood hallway they saw that on the walls on each side were embossed pictures of wild animals, lions, tigers, wolves, and bears. A hat stand to the right of them was made of bent wood, and a carved cobra wrapped around in coils spiralled all the way down to the base of it. After looking at it Bruce raised his eyebrow whiskers, pulled a face, and looked at Stevie, who gave a lopsided smile.

The entrance hall had been very grand once, but now the long deep-red diamond-patterned carpet looked threadbare. Oil paintings of ancestors hung on the staircase walls. Some were of what looked like elegant Spanish-looking women with thick, black hair woven in intricate jewel-covered buns with their husbands, who looked quite short in comparison to them.

"I'll tek you into the sitting room. Alwyn will put your cases in the bedrooms. Laddie, leave your case there. He'll come and get it for ye."

Relieved, Stevie did as he was told, and Mr Beavis, Bruce, Stevie, and Fergal followed behind the housekeeper into the sitting room. To Mr Beavis's horror, the housekeeper's dress under her apron had risen up at the back, due to the strain of her large belly, and a large pair of well-worn off-white bloomers hanging down her thick, bow-shaped stockinged legs was on display from the back.

Aware Fergal about to open his beak and say something about it, Mr Beavis nodded his head furiously at him from behind and signalled him not to speak. It seemed to do the trick and Fergal, under protest, remained silent, his beak twitching as he stifled a laugh. It was difficult to not look, though. Bruce, being the shortest, sadly had a bird's-eye view of Mrs Bucket's generous bottom.

After coming into the sitting room, she beckoned them to sit on wide, dark grey tapestried chairs. A fire had been lit in the enormous marble fireplace and red, gleaming coals choked out sparks of coal dust from the grate on to the carpet. Above the mantelpiece was an oil painting, which, it said below, was of Remus McFetrich, a heavily bearded man dressed in a black evening suit. In his hand was a dark brown wooden walking stick with a lion's head.

"Ah see ya all looking at Mr McFetrich. Grand man, he was. It was a sad day when he passed away," Mrs Bucket said. Sniffing into a handkerchief, she added, "You settle yourself down and I'll get ya some tea and scones."

Mr Beavis beamed at her as she went out of the door and pulled a long white envelope from his jacket pocket, which he opened. He proceeded to read the contents out loud to Fergal. It was the last will and testament of Remus McFetrich. Fergal already knew the contents of it, but Mr Beavis seemed keen to repeat it to him.

Fergal had been left Loch House in the will and all the McFetrich land, which included rented cottages.

"I have some papers for you to sign, but that can be done after dinner. I would like to be here for a short while with you, if I may."

"Stay as long as you like," yawned Fergal, scratching his beak and starting to get tired. He was also overwhelmed by all the responsibility that was about to fall on his feathered shoulders.

When Mrs Bucket returned they soon found out that her tea was rather weak and watery and her scones heavy, but everyone was starting to feel hungry and they all greedily gulped them down until nothing was left of them. With them now refreshed, she said,

"Ah, Alwyn, can you show the gentlemen to their rooms, please?"

A morose-looking Alwyn in the doorway nodded in reply. Everyone was keen to get to their bedrooms and sort themselves out, so they all stood up quickly when she spoke.

As they followed Alwyn up the heavily patterned red carpet they saw that the walls were lined with paintings of elephants, lions, and bears.

"In the old days, the master kept a lot of the wild beasts. Och, he did so love his pet lion," said Alwyn, coughing into a handkerchief, and noticing them all glancing at the paintings.

"My uncle kept a lion?" asked an incredulous Fergal.

"Och, aye … Bears, snakes, everything. You name it, laddie, he had them. But as he got older the animals became too much fur him

– always fighting, they were. Well, apart from the lion. He was far too gentle."

"Where did they live?"

"Round the back of the house, he had stables – even a bear pit – but the lion lived in the house. Watch ye don't fall down the bear pit there, though. If you're on your own you will never get oot of it, and you would be there forever. No one would ever find you and, who knows, there may be a ghostie of a bear doon there who will eat ya up." Alwyn laughed, as if the thought of the bird coming to some misfortune was an amusing one.

"Hmm … Very funny," came Fergal's sniffy, unamused reply.

As they reached the landing of the house an Egyptian sarcophagus in a glass frame stared creepily back at them. Unnerved, the group quickly followed behind Alwyn.

After opening a thick wooden door, Alwyn beckoned to Stevie.

"This is your room," he said. "I put your case on ya bed. Dinner is always at 7 p.m. That door there next to ya is the bathroom."

After looking at the opulent bedroom, Bruce smiled at Stevie.

"Wow. This is so cool."

The bedroom had a huge mahogany four-poster bed, surrounded by thick red curtains. To the left side of the door was an enormous painting of a brown eagle in flight, soaring over a snow-topped mountain. A large wooden dresser with an oval frame was in the centre of the room, with a china bowl and a jug of water. Next to it was a double wardrobe. To the back of the room was a fireplace with coal stocked up in a wooden box, fire tongs, and a poker hanging off a tool stand. The floor was covered with a gold- and red-patterned rug.

"I hope my bedroom is as good as this," Bruce said.

Stevie grinned back at Bruce and went to the bed to unpack his case.

"If you come with me, I'll tek ya to ya room," Alwyn continued.

Bruce turned eagerly and followed with Fergal and Mr Beavis, who had been admiring the paintings in the hallway. There was an impressive carved lion's head on the wood of the door he opened. Inside was a large wooden cage to the back of the room, but it had a strange smell – almost gamey. The bed was wide, with woollen blankets and a sheepskin rug adorning it, but it wasn't as luxurious as Stevie's room. It was quite a simple room. A wicker basket full of football-sized red knitted balls lay in a clumsily made heap. There was a dressing table with a cracked mirror, but it was lopsided and looked like it had been in the wars. A bowl and a jug of water lay beside it. A cracked, blocked-up fireplace finished off the room.

Bruce, puzzled and disappointed, looked around.

"This was Godric's bedroom."

"Godric?"

"Aye, Godric, the master's pet lion. With ya being a wee pussy I thought you would want ta play with Godric's red balls. I've put a bowl of milk by the wardrobe. You pussies love milk, don't ya?" Alwyn grinned good-humouredly. He ruffled Bruce's furry head and pointed at a red china bowl as he went out of the door.

A giggle came from behind him and Bruce, flustered, knew immediately that it was from Fergal. There came a stern look from Mr Beavis, and Fergal followed him out of the room still giggling.

He must think I'm one of those cats that play with balls and stuff, thought Bruce, scratching his left armpit in frustration, but the itch moved to his right armpit, making him look like he was about to start dancing samba-style. As he gazed around the room he saw deep scratch marks on all the furniture. It was hard to believe a lion had slept in this room, although there was a strong musky smell – what he would call a 'catty smell'.

To try and get rid of it he went around the room, rubbing his mouth on corners of the wall to exchange his scent for it. Then, after going over to the wicker basket, he picked up a red and green knitted football, gazed over his shoulder to make sure no one was there, placed it on the ground, and began pushing it cautiously with his paw around the room. It began happily bouncing off the walls and the wardrobe, and then finally went under the bed.

He purred and crawled under the bed, and pushed himself further under until he managed to reach it. A piece of paper was stuck to the football as he brought it out from under the bed. It looked like a diagram of a large black dog with strange symbols beside it. On the back of the piece of paper someone had written in spidery handwriting with a fountain pen:

None of the experiments worked, but we don't know why?.

Puzzled, he looked again at it, but it made no sense to him. He laid it on the dressing table and placed the football back in the wicker basket.

He sighed at his large, battered, and bulging case and went over to it. Bruce would much rather play with the ball, but he had to unpack his case. Besides, he had food that needed to go in the kitchen, and decided he would give the shortbread and the pound loaf to Mrs Bucket as a present instead of giving it to the others. As he bent forward he noticed his red jumper was covered in long, coarse golden hairs. After smelling them he gulped at realising what they were. Lion hairs.

Jeez. I hope that lion is definitely dead. I don't want it finding me in here if it comes back. It would have me as breakfast, he thought, trembling, but then a wave of common sense took over and he shook his head. The lion must be dead – surely, it must be. Wouldn't they have heard it roaring if it was still alive?

Now purring loudly, he began unpacking his case. Then, as an afterthought, he went over to the wardrobe, bent down, and began lapping up the slightly warm milk in the red bowl.

Fergal was also disappointed with his room. His bedroom was the room of his late uncle, Remus McFetrich. It had a huge bookcase, an unpretentious, sturdy-looking bed with striped red, green, and yellow blankets, a threadbare, rust-coloured rug, and a dressing table crammed with notebooks, pens, and pencils. On the floor were a china washbowl and a jug of water. The wardrobe door was closed, but the white sleeve of a shirt was jammed in the corner of it. A large table at the back of the room was filled with things that looked like specimens of animals and butterflies. The room also had a stale odour about it. There also appeared to be a yellow tooth on a piece of red satin cloth. No doubt his uncle's, he thought, which had become loose at some point. But why leave it here?

Taking notice of Fergal's annoyed face, Alwyn said,

"We did not want ta move anything. Me wife just dusted around things."

"Well, I will be going through things and a lot of this will be thrown away," came Fergal's snooty reply.

"If you want anything, let me know. Just press the bell above the door," replied Alwyn, ignoring the remark.

"We'll go into the drawing room before dinner," said Mr Beavis. "There are estate matters to go through."

Fergal nodded, and watched Mr Beavis follow Alwyn out of the door.

Mr Beavis, like Stevie, had also ended up with a luxurious bedroom. On one side of the room was a bookcase crammed right up to the top of the wall with books. The bed was a four-poster bed with red and gold silk drapes. Even the blankets were red and gold. The dressing table had a gentleman's comb, a face bowl, and a jug. A solid bar of soap and a razor lay in a silver pewter dish. But the comb would not be much use for Mr Beavis, as his hair seemed to be on the point of falling off the back of his head.

Oh, yes, this room will do most nicely, thought Mr Beavis, and smiled, feeling sure his room was by far the best. Even the bedpan under the bed was a red and gold china bowl.

He went through his case and took out an A4-sized leather case, which looked like it was crammed with papers. After glancing through them he picked up the ones that Fergal needed to sign and laid them on the bed. He then removed his jacket and shirt and, after filling the bowl with water on the dressing table, proceeded to wash his red, blotchy upper body with the soap and water. He dried himself with a rough cloth that was beside the jug of water.

He went through his case and picked out a black suit and a white dinner shirt with a grey silk waistcoat.

No doubt we would have to dress for dinner in a place like this, he thought. As he pursed his lips he thought of Stevie and Bruce, and thought that they would, not even change for dinner. Fergal, of course, would be wearing something appropriate for the evening meal, so he would not be too dressed up if he dressed in evening clothes for dinner.

At 7 p.m. the dinner gong sounded, followed by the strikes of the grandfather clock in the hallway. As Stevie, Bruce, and Fergal came downstairs, Fergal went down the stairs first. He was dressed in a black evening suit, with a dicky bow. On his feet were a shiny black pair of shoes. Bruce had changed into a blue jumper, but all Stevie had done was flatten his floppy hair with water.

"Good evening, gentlemen." Mrs Bucket was looking up the stairs as they came down, and she smiled up at them. "If you follow me, I will tek you into the dining room."

As they followed her they were relieved that she appeared to have pulled the back of her dress down.

Chapter 7

They came into a rectangle-shaped dining room with a long wooden table, which was covered with plates and cutlery. A bread basket was filled with home-made rolls, and a strong smell of soup wafted from the table from a china tureen. As they sat down Mrs Bucket handed the bread basket to them. While they took the warmed rolls, she then proceeded to ladle what looked like a greasy beef broth that seemed full of lard into china soup bowls.

As Bruce slurped at the soup, much to Mr Beavis's annoyance, the solicitor went through details of the estate on a document he held in his hand.

"I have a plan of the estate, names of tenants you will need to see and, of course, papers to sign. That can be done after dinner. There is a rather peculiar request in the will that your uncle's lion, Godric, is looked after. But, of course, this will must have been written when the lion was alive. Mr and Mrs Bucket have also been left money in the will, along with lifetime employment. I trust that will acceptable."

Fergal nodded then threw his head back and poured the entire contents of the soup bowl down his throat. He finished the hot soup long before anyone else, and then began on the bread.

As Mrs Bucket came later to clear the first course, Bruce, rustling two bags, handed them to her and said,

"This is for you. It's a fruit shortbread, which I hope you will like, and eh a pound cake."

Taking the present from him and peering into the bags, she beamed at him when she saw what he had given her..

"Och, they smell lovely. What a kind pussy ya are. I'll have some with Alwyn for our supper." After placing the soup bowls and bags on a tray, she disappeared out of the room. She then returned a couple of minutes later with warmed dinner plates with thick slices of undercooked roast pork on them. A bowl with new potatoes and a red-hot tray of roasted, singed vegetables followed, with a watery-looking gravy.

Later, after the group had struggled with the disappointingly tasteless dinner and Mrs Bucket's special undercooked and weak-flavoured fruit pudding with home-made lumpy custard, they made their way to the library.

"Can I wander around the house and grounds?" asked Stevie, seeing all the papers Mr Beavis was taking out of a briefcase and feeling it might be time to disappear.

"I think that would be a good idea. Fergal has a lot of paperwork to go through."

"I'll come with you," said Bruce, jumping into the conversation.

"OK, guys, see you later," relied Fergal, looking quite gloomy as he went into the library, followed by Mr Beavis.

Stevie and Bruce walked into the kitchen. The heat of the room made their eyes water.

"Do you need a hand with the dishes, Mrs Bucket?" asked Bruce.

"Oh no. Alwyn and I will sort them. You have a wander round," she beamed at him. She had already decided he was the nicest of the group, and she now had her sights set on spoiling him with her food.

Noticing a heavy oak door at the back of the kitchen, Stevie asked what was in the room.

"Och … That, laddie, it's just Master McFetrich's special room. I haven't had a chance to go through it, but you boys have a look in it to see if it needs tidying up. He always kept it locked and tidied it himself but, if you go doon, mind it always had a nasty smell coming from it. It seems to have gone away now, though. Watch you dinna bang your head, laddie, with ya being so tall, though, as you come doon the stairs."

After handing Stevie a key from a cracked brown teapot resting on a table, and a lantern, she turned her back to them and began washing greasy plates with some carbolic soap.

Stevie and Bruce opened the creaking door and went down the narrow stone steps. Lines of cobweb threads hung down from the ceiling and tickled Stevie's nose. He sneezed and brushed them away. In front of them, down the stairs, was a large wooden table with loose dusty papers lying in a thick pile on one side. While guiding the lantern to the table, Stevie half-tripped on something blocking his way. In the gloomily lit cellar he could see a large wooden box. As he bent down to look at it, Bruce screamed and he jumped up in fright.

"Oh, Jeez ... Look at that," Bruce half-whispered in a squeaky voice.

When they looked inside the large box, they came face to face with the body of an enormous black wolf. Its yellow glass eyes glared out of them from the stained glass covering the box. The wide mouth twisted in an unpleasant snarl.

"This is so creepy. It looks alive. Let's get out of here," Bruce whimpered.

"Oh, Bruce, it's a stuffed animal in a box. It won't hurt us. Don't worry, man. Let's have a look around. I just want to see what's written on these papers. Look at all those bottles. Fergal's uncle must have been some sort of scientist."

But the smell of dog – or, in their case, wolf – was making Bruce quite sick, and he covered his mouth and started to look a bit glassy-eyed. As the tabby cat looked around the room, he could see what was in some of the bottles.

"Oh ... Stevie, man, this is so horrible. Look, there are eyeballs in that jar, and what's this pink ... this ...? Aah! It's a tongue. Oh, God. It's like a witch's parlour. It's so gross. Oh, Stevie, let's get out of here."

"Yeah, OK. I must admit I feel queasy. But see these diagrams? He must have been experimenting with animals. But why?"

"I don't care. I just want to get out," wailed Bruce.

"Come on then, scaredy-cat, but we'll have to tell Fergal about this room." As Bruce raced ahead up the cellar steps, Stevie turned around to look at the room. As he went up the stairs, a black shape scuttled across the room. It was a large rat, and it appeared to be looking up at him. It showed no fear as it stared into his eyes, then scuttled away into the dark shadows.

Stevie shuddered and quickly followed Bruce up the dusty steps and closed the cellar door. Once they got back into the kitchen, Bruce firmly closed the cellar door behind him then checked again, ensuring that the door was definitely locked. Best to make sure, just in case that wolf wasn't dead, but just in a deep sleep. Wolves and snakes were his deepest fear.

"Mr McFetrich seems to have used the cellar as a laboratory. We found a dead wolf down there."

Mrs Bucket, who was now laying pastry on a pie dish, looked up at Stevie and said,

"Och, I wouldn't know about that. I was never allowed to go doon there. The master cleaned the cellar himself." But there was something in the way she said it that made Stevie not believe her. But seeing him look at her, she went into the pantry and did not come out until Stevie and Bruce had left the kitchen.

"She didn't want to talk about it. Did you notice that?" said Stevie.

"Yeah, I did man. A bit weird, if you ask me. How would you not know, if you were working in the kitchen, that he had a dead wolf in the cellar?"

"I think he must have been some type of scientist, but why would he need a wolf to experiment on? We'll have to mention it to Fergal. Come on, let's go outside. I think I need some air after being in that cellar."

Bruce nodded back and they went out through the back door.

With it still being light they could see all around them. A long wooden hut faced them.

"Come on, let's have a look inside there," said Bruce, tugging at Stevie's sleeve.

"Bruce, you are so nosy," said Stevie, but Bruce's curiosity got the better of him and he scampered over to the door of the hut. He turned the handle, but it wouldn't open.

"Darn, it's locked. Hang on. That window's open. Give me a bunk-up and I'll climb inside there."

Curious, Stevie lifted his pal up.

"Oh, Bruce, move your tail. I'm getting cat hairs in my eyes. I can't see."

Bruce moved his tail to one side, then slowly climbed into the window, breathing in as he forced the last part of his plump belly inside the room.

The room was full of damp-looking timber, which lay horizontally across the floor. Bruce landed with a thud on the ground. He saw that a bucket and a chest of drawers were blocking the door, so he pushed them to one side. The key was in the lock and, after turning it, he invited Stevie into the room. But something touched Bruce's tail. As he bent down to look, he was distracted by a toy wooden soldier in the dust. He then turned around to see what was touching him.

"Yuk. Look at that, Stevie."

The pair stared at what was lying on the ground.

It looked like the large skeleton of a dog.

"Do you think it was the family dog and Mr McFetrich never got around to burying it?"

"Must have been a dog of a hell of a size. Look at the length of it, and look at the teeth on it."

Bruce looked at the skull of the dog.

"Stevie, do you think it's another wolf? Oh, Jeez. Can you imagine if the place is overrun with wolves? What if they come in the house? They might try and eat us, and I bet they would get me first."

"Don't be daft. If there were wolves here we would hear them howling," said Stevie, trying to be brave but getting as spooked as Bruce.

"Stevie, look. There's another skeleton."

This one was even bigger than the first.

"This is so creepy. Come on. Let's get out of here," said Stevie, hurriedly dragging Bruce out of the door.

The back of the house was covered by thick trees and overgrown bushes. A strong wind had come up from nowhere, making the leaves blow wildly around them. It was starting to give them the creeps. Then came a tiny splatter of raindrops on their heads.

"Come on, let's go back to the library," said Stevie.

As they walked back, Bruce turned around and cocked his head.

"What's wrong?"

"Oh, nothing. Just thought I heard something." Bruce shook his head as if trying to shake something out of his ears. To him it sounded like the deep purring of a cat. But there was nothing there, and he shrugged and went back inside the house with Stevie.

When they were back in the house they walked into the library, where they saw Fergal seated at a card table, going through documents, a bored look in his eyes. He looked helplessly at them.

"Well, that's all the papers finalised," said Mr Beavis. Loch House is now yours, along with the farm cottages. I will introduce you to the tenants tomorrow and that will be my job done. Your uncle did, as I mentioned before, wish for you to keep the services of Mr and Mrs Bucket and ensure the tenants would be allowed to stay in their cottages, as we discussed when I read the will out to you. I think that is everything concluded, and tomorrow I will go home."

After carefully rolling up the piece of parchment paper and tying it with a ribbon, Mr Beavis smiled and took off his glasses and rubbed his eyes. It had been a long day, and everyone was starting to feel very tired. So nobody argued when it was suggested that everyone should go to bed.

Bruce practically raced up the stairs to his bedroom, beating everyone else. But he did not sleep well at first. His wool blankets kept coming off the bed, and he felt that something or someone was pulling them off him. Annoyed, he opened his eyes, but he saw nothing.

Eventually, he fell into a deep sleep, half-purring his favourite song – 'The Rose of Tralee' – which now reminded him of the cat baker, Callie McFarrell, and her lovely green eyes.

But the song was taken over by something … something that caused the curtains to billow in the room. It was the purr of a very large cat, which had wandered into his room and settled itself on his bed. This time, with a tug, it took its share of the blankets, leaving a small corner for Bruce, but the little cat was sound asleep and oblivious to this.

The next morning, after a breakfast of lumpy porridge followed by steaming hot bacon, eggs, and burnt sausages in the breakfast room, Mr Beavis, while pouring the tea from a silver teapot at the breakfast table, mentioned the tenants again. One was a Bert Whedon and another was a lady called Marissa McKay. Fergal would not be able to see them as they were not on the island, according to Mrs Bucket. Mr Beavis then spoke the names of the families they needed to follow up so quickly that Fergal had forgotten half of them by the time he finished the sentence.

"I am afraid you will have to meet the tenants when they return to the island. I will not, of course, be here, but I am sure Mr and Mrs Bucket will introduce you to them."

"Is there anyone else you know of on the island?"

"Eh, well, no. The church is now deserted. A lot of the islanders have moved away. Robert Pugh, the minister, had an illness and, according to Mrs Bucket, whom I spoke to this morning, enjoys the solitude of the island. The strange thing is that he appears to have gone against his religion. Mrs and Mrs Bucket do not know why."

"Fergal, we found some skeletons of dogs in the hut outside last night, but they seemed to be very large dogs. It was really weird," burst in Bruce, feeling if he did not mention this strange sight he would burst.

"Skeletons?"

"Yes, but that's not all. In the cellar there's a huge wolf in a case and papers that look like your uncle was experimenting on animals."

"What? Uncle McFetrich? Whatever for?"

"We asked Mrs Bucket, but she didn't want to talk about it."

"Well, maybe you should leave this matter well alone if that is the case," broke in Mr Beavis drily. He did not want any unnecessary stress. In his mind, he had delivered his client to Howly Island and had him sign the papers, and now he wanted to just go home and sit in his comfortable brown leather armchair and smoke his pipe. If there was a mystery going on at Loch House, he did not want to hear about it.

A knock on the door interrupted the conversation, which was a relief for Mr Beavis.

Mrs Bucket entered the breakfast room.

"Sir, there is a lady and her sister here to see you."

Fergal didn't at first look up. He was staring, fascinated by the ornate sugar tongs in the silver sugar bowl, but a nudge from Stevie made him realise that Mrs Bucket was calling him sir and addressing him.

"Who are they?"

"Myra Bloodvein and her sister, Clarinda."

Everyone groaned when they heard this, apart from Mr Beavis, who thought it might be a rich new client he could place on his books.

"Oh, how nice of her to pop in, Fergal. You should meet her. I am sure she will know a lot about this island. It will be your first visitor to the house."

"Uh, well, I suppose so," replied Fergal cautiously. He didn't like her and couldn't understand why she would come to his house. Most of all, he was still annoyed that she had tried to buy both him and Bruce for her horrible child.

Just as he said this, the breakfast room door burst open and in marched Myra Bloodvein, her dress rustling as she moved.

"I apologise for the intrusion," she said, looking at each and everyone in the room. "I simply had to come and see you all. I hope you do not think this rude of me," she smiled, her voice quite shrill as she spoke.

"Oh, most certainly not, madam," replied Mr Beavis, beaming at her like she was a delightful pork chop.

Myra Bloodvein smoothed her dress down. She was dressed in a pearl-buttoned navy riding dress. On top of her head rested a small round riding hat in navy, with a white flower on the side of it. But it was her dark hair that was the most dramatic. It seemed to have grown and changed colour in the short space of time since they had seen her. It was piled luxuriously upwards in a mass of auburn waves. A riding crop was in her left hand as she removed her thick leather gloves and shook everyone's hand with her heavily ringed long fingers. Mrs Bucket, however, was ignored, so she quietly walked out of the room and bumped into a lady who seemed to have been outside the door.

"Oh, this is my sister, Clarinda." Myra introduced a short, grey-haired lady with a thick, tight bun on top of her head. She appeared to have a similar figure to Mrs Bucket. Where Myra's eyes seemed cold, this lady's eyes had a twinkle in them, and when she smiled, deep dimples appeared across her plump, rosy cheeks.

"Pleased to meet you all." Clarinda spoke softly in a Scottish accent. She was dressed in a green checked riding suit with a sage green shawl wrapped around her shoulders. Her grey-blue eyes sparkled as she gave everyone a hug. They warmed instantly to her, except Mr Beavis, who did not like what he termed 'unnecessary displays of affection'.

Another person who was not happy was Myra. She was not used to her sister getting all the attention and she glared at her jealously and said, not smiling,

"Shall we go into the sitting room?"

"Oh, have you been to my uncle's house before?"

"Oh, yes. Did I not mention that, before you took over the house, your uncle used to hold dinner parties? I was invited to many of them, so you see I know this house better than all of you." Myra gave a smug, superior laugh as she spoke back to the cormorant, then turned her back on him. Mr Beavis then gallantly, with a flourish, led both her and her sister into the sitting room.

Fergal, Stevie, and Bruce looked at one another, and Fergal raised his eyebrows.

"You would think it was her house, the way she is behaving," he whispered sulkily.

"I know. She sure is bossy," Bruce said in a low voice, shaking his head.

"Well, one thing's for certain. Once Mr Beavis has gone, I will not be letting her come back to the house. I don't like her at all. After all, this is my house," said Fergal, petulantly puffing up his chest feathers in agitation as he spoke.

Once in the sitting room, Myra sat on the larger tapestried two-seater, along with her sister.

"Now that we are neighbours I thought it right that I should offer you my help in any way I can."

"Why do I need your help?" asked Fergal, not caring if he was being rude.

"Well, I am sure, young man, you want to know more about this island and the people. If you are to run Loch House and oversee the estate management of the land, I am sure it would be useful to you for me to show you around the island."

"That is most kind of you, Myra. I am sure Fergal will find your advice most helpful," said Mr Beavis, embarrassed and feeling he could strangle Fergal if the bird lost him the chance of getting a rich client on his books.

"Thank you. It would be a great help if you could tell me more about the island, but, please, you do not need to show me around. After all, I can ask Mr and Mrs Bucket to help me." Fergal gave a sweet smile as he looked into the cold eyes of Myra Bloodvein, well aware that he had annoyed her.

"I would have thought you would want to be shown the island by a historian, but if you prefer the Buckets, with what I presume would be their limited education, well, that's your choice." Myra gave a slight snigger as she said this then continued speaking, saying, "The island was called Holy Island hundreds of years ago, but the islanders changed the name to Howly Island."

"Why did they do that?" Fergal asked.

"Oh, there was a religious fool, John Mullay, who tried to force the villagers to attend church. He failed. The islanders did not and still do not believe in God. He came to an unfortunate end with his meddling."

"What happened?"

"He was thrown into a wolf pit and eaten alive by wolves."

"Ugh … That is horrible," responded Bruce, visibly shocked.

"Well, he should have minded his own business." Myra gave a short, shrill laugh and seemed amused by the thought, brushing an invisible crumb off her lap as she spoke.

"Do the islanders not worship God, then?" Mr Beavis asked.

"Oh no, of course not. They have their own forms of worship."

"And what are they?"

But Myra would not be drawn into it and just replied,

"Any Christian worship is frowned upon on the island. There is a minister on the island, but he has gone quite mad and people just ignore him. It would be wise not to interfere with the islanders' beliefs. In fact, it would be better to embrace them."

"Embrace atheists?"

"Yes."

There was an embarrassing silence, and Mr Beavis decided not to be drawn any further into the matter.

"My uncle kept a lion. Did you ever see it?"

"Oh, yes, Fergal. Stupid creature. He spoilt it. The animal had no brain. It had the run of the house."

"Were you not frightened of it?"

"I think it was more frightened of me," came Myra's derisory answer.

"Did it ever eat anyone?"

Just as Bruce asked this question, Mrs Bucket came in, asking if she should serve tea. Fergal nodded back.

"Godric eat anyone? Indeed not. He would never have harmed anyone," said Mrs Bucket, answering Bruce back indignantly, her teacups clattering as she set them down. "He was lovely, followed the master everywhere, loved my fried breakfasts, and always had a bowl of tea and piece of ma seed cake." She started to sniff as she spoke, and got a floral handkerchief out of her pocket.

"What happened to him?" asked Bruce.

"Someone poisoned him."

"Oh, Mrs Bucket, don't be silly. He was an old lion. He died of old age."

"No, he did not, madam ... and he was not an old lion. He was very young, and I saw him when he died. I know poisoning when I see it. I tell you, some evil person poisoned him. The master went downhill after that."

"I hardly think a housekeeper would know if an animal had been poisoned. I therefore suggest you keep your suspicions to yourself, or you will find yourself in a great deal of trouble."

Mrs Bucket lowered her head, sniffed into her handkerchief, and went to walk out of the room, but was stopped by Fergal, who patted her hand with his own white-feathered one.

"Wait, Mrs Bucket. Please do not go. Myra, I would prefer it if you did not speak to my housekeeper in such a rude manner."

As she turned her long neck around in amazement, Myra could only splutter, her face red with rage. It was obvious that she wanted to say something else, but had decided against it. Instead, she swallowed and said,

"I just wanted to assure your housekeeper that the lion had not been poisoned. I came to be a friend and to offer you my help. Are you sure you do not wish me to show you around the island?" She spoke in a slightly hurt tone and looked at Mr Beavis with sad-looking eyes.

"Eh, no thanks. I'll go around the island with my friends in my own time. I like finding places. I am good at that." He said it in such a pleasant way, but his beak twitched as he spoke and Stevie knew he was stifling a laugh.

"Very well. That is your choice, but Howly Island is quite wild and you may get lost. The weather changes very quickly around here. There have even been accounts of locals who have been found dead after losing their way." Myra twirled a corner of her dress collar as she spoke, carefully saying the word 'dead' to him with emphasis, as if to frighten him. Then she stood up rather stiffly and said,

"Well, I must be off. I will have to forego the tea. I have an acquaintance I need to meet on an important matter. I have my carriage outside."

She shook Mr Beavis's hand, but as he tried to speak to her she walked quickly to the door and completely ignored Bruce, Stevie, and Fergal. She was followed by Mrs Bucket and her flustered sister, Clarinda, who quickly hugged everyone and turned to Fergal to say,

"Your uncle was a very nice man. He helped so many people and was so kind to animals. I liked him a lot. Such a shame he passed away. And, as for Godric, he was a lovely lion … so gentle. What a beautiful creature he was. I used to love to stroke his soft fur."

"Clarinda, come on." Myra turned around, annoyed. Her mouth pursed as she looked at her sister walking out of the door. Clarinda flustered and, after apologising to everyone, swiftly followed her.

"I don't think Myra was too pleased with you, Fergal."

"I know, Stevie, but she was so rude to Mrs Bucket. I don't like her, and at least she will not come to call again. I thought Clarinda was really nice, didn't you?"

"Yeah, so different from her sister. You wouldn't think they were related."

70

"You may regret not accepting her kind invitation, Fergal. This is a large island. You could get lost," said Mr Beavis, cutting into the conversation. He sighed, realising he had lost a valuable client, and then he stood up briskly. "Well, Fergal, Mrs Bucket has arranged a carriage for me. It is due shortly. Her husband has taken my case downstairs. I have, as instructed in the will, read the contents of the safe and, as well as the estate, you now have all monies belonging to your late uncle. I will take my leave from you and I wish you every success in your new home. A final bill will be forwarded to you in due course." As he shook the bird's hand he even smiled at Bruce and Stevie, then left the room, and they could hear him shouting out to Mrs Bucket, asking for his coat.

"Well, you are master of all this, Fergal. Man, this is so cool. You could get lost in this house."

"I know, Bruce. What a place. You will stay a while with me, won't you, guys?"

"Of course, Fergal. No worries there," Stevie and Bruce said in unison.

"Thanks, guys." But Fergal's blue eyes looked sad when he said this, and Bruce sensed that moving to Howly Island was maybe not as great as Fergal had once thought.

"We'll come and see you, and you know you will always be welcome at Mum and Dad's."

"I know, Stevie," came Fergal's reply, but his eyes became wet-looking, as if tears had quickly come into them. When he saw them looking, he looked away and said loudly, "Come on, let's go and find Mr Bucket and see if he can show us around the island."

Bruce looked at Stevie and they both felt sad for their friend. They knew his life would now never be the same.

71

Chapter 8

Mr Bucket was busy peeling potatoes in the kitchen and, after taking his hands out of the sloppy brown water, he wiped them on a tea towel and said in reply to Fergal asking if he would take them around the island, that if they gave him five minutes he would get the horse and trap.

"You can finish what you are doing. We are in no hurry, Mr Bucket."

"No, sir. Best do it now, just in case the weather changes for the worse"

"Oh eh okay."

Mr Bucket then went out of the room.

"Do you think we need our coats Fergal?"

"No, it seems quite warm Stevie," The bird then began flapping his wings, and pecking at his tail feathers.

"I'll prepare a cold lunch for ya when ya get back," shouted Mrs Bucket, coming down the stairs and smiling at them as they went out of the door.

"Thanks," Fergal replied and waddled out of the door, followed by Stevie and Bruce.

The old horse, Ralph, who was leading the trap, was an old Clydesdale, a Goliath of a horse and exceptionally strong. But, again, it was another animal, to Bruce's immense disappointment, that did not speak.

Stevie, Fergal, and Bruce climbed into the trap. Bruce began having difficulty climbing up so was given a bunk-up by Stevie. As they wiped down the cobwebs on the seating, Mr Bucket said,

"The horse and trap have not been used for a long time and are only used to collect deliveries."

"Yes, I can see," replied Fergal, pulling a face as he got his green handkerchief out of his breast pocket to dust the seat in case it marked his fine clothes.

"Aye, it dinna come out much. I canna remember the last time Ralph went out on a long journey. One of the wheels needs a canny bit of attention, but I'll sort that out. Oh, here, you'll need to put these round ya to make sure you're all right."

He handed them a garlic garland each and proceeded to put one around the neck of the horse, and opened his shirt to reveal a silver cross. Seeing them looking puzzled, he said,

"Morgana vampire bats. They come out sometimes in the middle of the day. It used to be only at night, but they seem to be getting stronger. Now they come out at all hours."

"Oh no holy kittens.. Here we go again. Jeez i don't know if I want to go out after all," Bruce wailed out and rubbed his furry forehead in agitation.

"Och, they'll be all right. So lang as ya have the garlic they leave ya alone."

"What happens if you don't have the garlic Mr Bucket?"

"They drain ya blood and ya die, laddie."

Stevie looked at Bruce and Fergal and shook his head in disbelief at them.

"Is there no way you can kill them?"

"Well, ya uncle did try and make potions to throw at them, but they never worked. If anything, they seemed ta get stronger. You'll be all right with the garlic. All the islanders use it. The vampire bats tend more to go for humans. Birds and animals are second best fur them, so I should think you and the wee pussy will be all right, but best to make sure."

"Oh, great. Looks like Mr Bucket and I are the only ones who are likely to get bitten. But I still think we should go around the island, Fergal, because you need to see where you are going to live."

"Stevie, I am not sure if I want to live here after hearing this."

"Oh, don't be like that. As Mr Bucket says, as long as you have the garlic, we'll be all right. Come on. We can't stay cooped up in the house. How boring would that be?"

"I suppose you're right, although I am surprised Myra didn't mention them when she visited us."

"Och ... they wouldn't go near her, that's why. That woman would terrify them."

73

"You are joking, aren't you?"

"No, I'm not. She's a bad woman and that's no mistake, ah can tell ya. She'd be sucking their blood, and dinna think I'm joking about it."

"Oh, what makes her so bad?"

"She has wronged people: she is so different from her sister. Why, even the wee lassie is starting to get like her. Myra Bloodvein has brought bad luck to Oban and Howly since she's been here, and no mistake. Och ... Well, I'll show ya the island. There are some lovely things ta see."

Mr Bucket, after taking up the reins, made clicking noises to the horse. It slowly started moving its huge Clydesdale body forward. The carriage passed an old abandoned school. Mr Bucket told them there were no children on the island. Families, he said, had moved to the Isle of Skye.

"No children? So who does live on the island?"

"Farmers, the minister, ya tenants, and gipsies and other folks who tend ta keep to themselves."

Fergal shook his head in reply.

"Och, it's not so bad. Joe Plump is one of the farmers. We'll hopefully get ta meet him. He'll be a good friend fur ya."

After rounding a bend, the carriage twisted around tree-lined corners, and led to a long dirt track shrouded by hedgerows.

"Ah, he's in. The geese are oot."

The horse trotted up to a ramshackle cottage, which smelt strongly of manure, then stopped and everyone got out. Mr Bucket picked up the brass knocker. It did not make a noise at first. On the second knock it boomed out, resulting in a film of paint coming loose and falling off the door. Guiltily, he rubbed away the evidence of this.

The door opened and a face peered out.

"Hello, Joe. Just introducing ya to Fergal, the new landowner of Loch House."

"Well, well, well. A bird. The new owner of Loch House. That will ruffle a few feathers with folks, hee-hee. Please to meet ya, Fergal." The farmer laughed at his own joke, his double chin wobbling as he rubbed his rather dirty face. He was a short man with a full ginger beard, which poured down his stained green smock. His thick dark wool trousers were tucked into a pair of muddy, thick-soled boots.

"Hello," said Fergal, shaking his hand.

"The master would like ta see the new tenants, but I believe they are away," interrupted Mr Bucket.

"Aye, I believe they are, though some say they have done a runner and you will no be getting your rent." The farmer laughed again.

"Who said that?" asked Mr Bucket.

"Och, just gossip. Dinna tek any notice of me, laddie. They must just be away. We must talk business when you're sorted. I have the best fruit and veg and beef stock around here. Mrs Bucket gets her meat from me." The farmer smiled at Fergal.

"Who are these two?" the farmer then asked.

"This is Stevie Rump and the pussy is called Bruce, and would ya believe this pussy talks?" Mr Bucket laughed as he spoke, and stroked Bruce's head.

Stevie and Bruce then shook the bemused farmer's hand.

"We are just staying with our friend until he gets sorted," said Bruce.

"Och, he speaks. You were right. Hee-hee. A talking pussy. Heh-hch. And what a voice. Are you from the Americas?"

"The Caribbean."

"Oh, aye, same thing. Och, well, any friend of the new owner of Loch House is a friend of mine. The more people and talking animals coming ta the island the better, what with so many folks leaving."

"Why are they leaving the island?" Stevie asked.

"Why, because of the monsters, of course."

"Monsters?"

"Aye. I have never seen them, but there are people who have and lived to tell the tale. They say they come out of the sea and eat people."

"Dinna be frightening the master with ya daft tales, Joe."

"Aye, he's right. Tek no notice of me. Ye will be fine living here."

"Eh, I am sure I will," said Fergal, but he sounded decidedly unsure and was starting to feel very nervous about the island and Loch House and wondering what he had come to.

"Well, Joe, we'll be off. I'll share a wee dram with ya next time I see ya."

"Aye, ya will. Well, pleased ta meet ya all. My wife is at the bottom of the field. She will be sorry to have missed a talking pussy. Heh-heh. Whatever next!" He finished his sentence with a high-pitched laugh and Bruce gave a strained smile, but he was getting fed up with being called a talking pussy.

After saying their goodbyes, they climbed back on to the trap. The horse twitched his tail, and began moving. The journey took them further around the island, past a windmill and some crofters' cottages, and Mr Bucket pointed over to an area completely covered in flowers.

"See there? That's the faerie glen. You can make a wish there if ya want teh. If the faerie likes ya, he makes it come true."

"Have you ever made a wish, Mr Bucket?" Stevie asked, excitedly.

"Aye, but I dinna think the faerie liked me, as I got nothing. See over there? That's the start of the Bonhomie Caves. Many a fisherman has drowned himself there. Not a nice place. Full of mermaids from the Black Sea. They are a nasty bunch, are the Fee Sisters, and their cronies, the Sand Witches."

"The Fee Sisters?"

"Aye. A big family, but rotten. All of 'em. Keep well away from them, and if ya walk on the beach watch oot for the Sand Witches. Ah hear they drag ya into the sea to drown."

"My word. Whatever next!"

But no one responded to Fergal. They were too busy trying to make themselves comfortable in the carriage.

Chapter 9

The horse trotted quickly towards the distance, and almost at once there seemed to be a dark grey cloud looming over an area ahead of them.

"What's over there?" Stevie pointed his finger past the whirling mass, which was moving forward to a long black shadow of trees.

"Och. That horrible place? It's the Howling Forest. I never go there."

"Are there any places I can go to around here that are safe?" Fergal asked, sounding completely fed up now and making eye contact with Stevie and Bruce, who were starting to look worried about Fergal's new home.

"Aye, there're good places, ya just hev to find them. I'll show ya. Dinna ya worry yourself. Come on, Ralph, move yourself. What ya stopping fur? Well, look up at the sky. It's a clear day. Looks like the vampire bats are staying in the Howling Forest, so it dinna look like any of you need to worry yourselves. See, it's not always bad on the island. Why, ya have been lucky. Last week it never stopped raining. Was like a mermaid's picnic, it was. Look at it now. Very bonny island it is."

No one answered. All of them were looking up at the sky, just double-checking they were not surrounded by vampire bats. But the horse stood still and refused to move until Mr Bucket gave him a carrot. The horse, after accepting the bribe, began crunching on it and then moved forward again.

After they passed the beach, they finally ended up back at the house. Outside the house was Mrs Bucket with a young white seagull dressed in an Arran jumper two sizes too big for him. Catching sight of them, the housekeeper waved and brushed down her billowing pinny.

"Ah, there's wee Stewie, my nephew. Hi there, laddie," shouted Mr Bucket to the waving bird.

"Hello," the seagull mouthed back.

"Finally, a talking bird," said Bruce excitedly.

As they dismounted the trap, Mr Bucket introduced the young seagull to them. Fergal and the bird rubbed beaks and the young seagull said,

"I've heard a lot about ya, sir. Nice to meet ye."

Fergal smiled back. The bird had such a friendly smile with a wide grin you could not help but like, but whatever was he wearing? The jumper was trailing on the ground, it was so long, and some of the wool had become undone on the hem.

"Hey, you two are so alike. Why, you could be brothers," said Bruce, coming closer to the pair. "Why, Stewie even has a scar on his beak, just like you."

Bruce was right. Even though they were a different species of bird they were so alike, even down to height and weight and to the tail feathers.

"Of course, Stewie is better-looking than you," said Stevie, mischievously.

"He doesn't have your sticky-out belly," added Bruce, staring in fascination at them.

"Shut up, guys."

"Stewie, ignore them."

"These two are quite mad."

The seagull laughed and proceeded to pull his jumper down, which resulted in him nearly falling over. Fergal caught him before he fell, and asked,

"Have you not got anything smaller to wear? You are going to break your neck wearing that."

"No, I have nae clothes. My suitcase with my clothes in got blown away on the fishing boat I was travelling in. My uncle lent me this jumper."

"Oh, we can't have that. Leave it with me. You can have some of my clothes. After all, we are about the same size. I'll go through my things after lunch."

"Och, that's very kind of ya."

Bruce looked at the two and smiled back at the seagull.

"Are you staying long at Loch House?"

"Well, my uncle's asked me to help with the estate as his back is not as good as it was, especially for the chopping of wood and planting seeds. I can stay as long as he wants me if ya are happy with that, sir."

"Of course. You can stay as long as you like. If Mr and Mrs Bucket have this arrangement, I am not going to change it. Besides, I would be grateful for the company."

Fergal was thinking he would be very lonely after Stevie and Bruce went home. It would be nice to have someone near to his own age on the estate to keep him company.

"That's very kind of ya, sir." Mr Bucket was delighted when he heard this.

"No problem at all, and don't call me sir. Call me Fergal," replied Fergal as Mr Bucket went to unharness Ralph and put the trap away.

"Hello, Mrs Bucket."

Mrs Bucket smiled at Bruce and, after touching his face, said,

"Why, you are frozen, you poor wee pussy. Come inside with me. You will catch your death. You should have been wearing your coat." She grabbed Bruce and, oblivious to the others, hurried him into the house. She was followed by Stevie and Stewie, who looked at each other and grinned.

"Everyone is like that with Bruce. They fall in love with him and want to pet and look after him," whispered Stevie to Stewie.

"Hmm … They do. He gets very spoilt," replied Fergal, slightly jealously.

As they came into the house they could smell cooking.

"If you wash your hands and then sit yourselves doon in the dining room I'll serve you lunch."

"Have some lunch with us, Stewie, and tell us a bit about yourself," said Fergal, sounding more mature than he really was.

"Thank ya. I will," the excited young bird beamed back at them.

After coming back from washing their hands, they came downstairs and, in the dining room, they saw that Mrs Bucket had prepared a strange flour soup, but it looked like some of the flour was floating in lumps on the top of it. Uneven slices of white bread lay on a china plate. Everyone grabbed the bread, hoping the soup

79

would be more appetising soaked into the bread. The bread was quite hard, but everyone ate it rather than offending Mrs Bucket.

As she came in to clear the greasy bowls, she said,

"Oh, I nearly forgot. There was a gentleman caller who came when you were out. Very tall. Said his name was Wallace Whiskerman – a cheetah, would ya ken that? Very smartly dressed, well-spoken. Said he was an inspector of police from London, of all places."

"Where is he now?"

"Och, he said he had ta see someone and would call again."

"I wonder what he wants. A police inspector from London coming here … whatever for?"

"What have you been doing, Fergal?" said the tabby cat mischievously, as he licked his striped paw and washed his face.

"It's not me, Bruce, he'll be after. It will probably be about you using a bowl of trifle as a dangerous weapon to throw at the Queen of England."

"Oh no," the little cat wailed back. The joke had reverberated back on him.

"Don't talk rot, Fergal. Bruce, it won't be anything to do with that. Mum sorted it. It will be about something completely different."

"Oh, Stevie, do you think so?"

"Of course, you silly goose. Stop worrying about that. It's long forgotten."

The next course served was what looked like a savoury cheese custard with boiled potatoes and cabbage. This too was very bland. The final course was a squashed-looking pink apple jelly.

Bruce and Fergal gave each other knowing looks. It was obvious that Fergal was going to have to teach Mrs Bucket how to cook, and also how to add flavour to food.

"Stewie, where are you from?"

"Aviemore. I received a letter from my uncle and came over to help oot."

"Do you go to school?"

"No, sir, I left school at fourteen to help look after my ma and sisters. My da died and I had to support them. My ma does not make much with her sewing and cleaning jobs. I send some of the money ma uncle gives me back to her."

"Well, as I said before, you can stay here as long as you want and if you help your uncle, you would be a great help to me. Oh, hang on … I have just remembered. I need to pay the wages – another thing Mr Beavis reminded me about. I will sort them after lunch for you and your uncle and aunt. You will, I believe, all need to sign for them."

"Aye, that's right."

During the rest of the meal Fergal thought the conversation was too much about Stewie and proceeded to tell him about their adventures in the Caribbean, to his amazement and delight. This was not so exciting for Stevie and Bruce, though, who had heard it all before, and most of it was exaggerated to make Fergal into some sort of superhero.

Later, with the dishes cleared away by Mrs Bucket, Fergal went upstairs with Stewie to find some clothes for him. An hour later, as they walked on the landing, a smartly dressed Stewie asked Fergal,

"Fergal, can I show ma clothes to my uncle?"

"Of course you can," replied Fergal, pleased and full of self-congratulation that he had managed to turn Stewie into a sophisticated country gent. Stewie was dressed in a brown tweed short-legged suit, with gaiters holding up thick pea-green ribbed socks. On his head was a tweed cap, which hung over one of his blue eyes. But on his webbed feet were his old, battered shoes, which did not match the fine clothes. Fergal frowned and made a mental note that he would have to buy Stewie a couple of pairs of shoes.

Stevie, who was walking behind the pair on the stairs, said, after Stewie excitedly ran down the stairs and out of the front door,

"Hey, Fergal, he won't be able to wear that tweed suit when he helps his uncle. Won't he be doing manual work?"

"Yes, he will, but I just wanted to give him something nice. I have some of my uncle's jumpers I can give him in the old trunk in his room. My uncle went very thin, by the looks of it, judging by the size of the clothes he had, and I think they might still be a bit loose, but will fit him. I might give him the lot," he replied kindly.

Stevie nodded back and smiled. He was not interested in Fergal's fancy clothes. The different styles Fergal wore were lost on him. He much preferred to wear baggy shirts and trousers, and sometimes didn't even tuck in his shirts.

After following Bruce into the library, he watched Fergal struggle to open a most strange-looking safe. It was a light grey and looked like a Rayburn oven on wheels.

"Do you need a hand?"

"No, I've got the right combination. Ah, this is … it isn't half tight, though." The cormorant finally opened the safe door. Some white envelopes with Mr and Mrs Bucket's and Stewie's names on for their wages were on top of the papers, and Fergal grabbed them and took them out. There were also some bags of money, tied in brown sackcloth. Fergal looked at them and turned to Stevie.

"Can you help me go over the safe book and housekeeping ledger while you are here? You are really good at maths, and I just haven't a clue. I didn't want to look stupid in front of Mr Beavis."

"Yeah, no worries, but y' know you could afford to pay someone to do your books when I'm not here. Hey, where's Bruce?"

"Oh, he's giving some recipes to Mrs Bucket."

"He's brave, but I bet he has her following them. He will wrap her around his little paw. Hey, we might get some good food now."

"Oh, I hope so. That flour soup nearly finished me off … Ugh." Fergal gave an exaggerated groan and held his stomach in mock agony.

"Yeah, it was pretty bad, but she is such a nice lady. I'm sure both you and Bruce will get her cooking some of your good stuff. Hey, Fergal, look. There's a book on the Caribbean here. See … Looks good, doesn't it?"

Fergal shut the safe door and Stevie handed him the book, which was beautifully illustrated. As they flicked through the pages, the door opened and Bruce came in.

"Well, the deed is done, guys. Mrs Bucket has made a lovely fish pie – with my help, of course – and I have made my special marmalade pudding. We have made, would you believe, my version of a clootie dumpling? I know it's not Hogmanay, but I really wanted to make this recipe."

"Well done, Bruce," replied Fergal, beaming at him. "Real food at last. I knew you could do it."

"Thanks. I've even put silver threepenny bits in the dumpling for luck, to celebrate Fergal's new home. There are, I noticed, some great handwritten recipe books, maybe from the previous housekeeper, in one of the bookcases. But a warning, guys: Mrs Bucket made some rock buns yesterday, one of which I tried and nearly broke one of my front teeth. So, if she offers you one, I would dunk it in a cup of tea or you'll have no teeth left."

"But, hey, guys, my first attempt at getting her to cook decent food has been a great start. I have even shown her the art of seasoning food."

Bruce beamed at his cleverness and gave Fergal a high five with his paw.

"Oh, Bruce, real food ... I still feel sick, thinking about that flour soup."

"Me too. But hey, Fergal, between us we'll get her cooking some great food."

"Oh, I so hope so."

A voice outside the door became louder and finally the door opened and Mr Bucket peeped round it.

"Have ya seen wee Stewie?"

"I thought he had gone to find you, to show you his clothes."

"Och, has he? I'll go and look outside. Maybe he's round one of the outhouses."

Mr Bucket shut the door behind him.

"Bruce, look at this book on the Caribbean. It's great."

Stevie passed the book to Bruce, who began pawing it and slightly scratching the paper with his claws as he turned the pages.

"Yeah, you'll like it. There's a parrot fish that looks just like you," said Fergal cheekily.

"Very funny," replied Bruce, pulling a face and refusing to take the bait.

As the three of them looked at the book, it reminded them of St Lucia and made them feel quite sad and homesick. So engrossed were they that they did not at first notice the door open and a worried-looking Mr Bucket appeared. His face was quite pale and his voice wavered as he spoke.

"Sir, I canna find the lad. I have looked everywhere. My wife has been all over the house."

"Stewie might have just gone for a walk. We'll come and help you look. He must be somewhere. Don't worry. We'll find him," replied Fergal, giving a puzzled look and putting the book down.

"Thank you, sir. But if he had gone for a walk, why didn't he say?"

Nobody could answer his question, so they all went outside, shouting Stewie's name loudly. But there was no sign of him.

"Have you checked the cellar, Mr Bucket? He might be locked in there."

"Aye, laddie. My wife did."

A tear-stained Mrs Bucket came outside, dabbing at her nose with a floral handkerchief.

"If anything has happened to the laddie ..." she began to say, but Mr Bucket shushed her.

"Dinna ya worry, lassie. We'll find him," he said, putting a huge arm round her shoulders. But still they couldn't find him. It was as if he had disappeared into thin air.

"Mr Bucket, get the horse and trap out, please. We'll do a search further out of here. If he went for a walk, he might have got lost."

"Aye, sir." Mr Bucket hurried off to the stable, harnessed his horse, and attached him to the trap.

"Bruce, can you stay here and look after Mrs Bucket?" asked Fergal.

"Sure," came Bruce's reply, knowing really it was to calm down Mrs Bucket, whose crying was getting louder. "Come inside, Mrs Bucket. I will make you a nice cup of tea. I'm sure they'll find him." The little cat spoke gently to the housekeeper and guided her back into the house as the other three set off in the horse and trap.

"Put on the garlic garlands. I see the sky is getting dark. It could be just rain coming, but it might be vampire bats coming oot."

Everyone did as they were told and then Ralph trotted, screwing up his nose in displeasure at having to go out again. There were no bats in sight, but everyone kept the garlands on just in case they appeared.

Finally they came to Joe Plump's farm. He was busy tying up bales of hay and waved to them as they came on to his land.

"Hello, Joe. Have you seen my wee nephew Stewie?"

"Och, you know I thought I did. Was he not going out in Mrs Bloodvein's black carriage? I recognised the winged crest of the serpent on the side of it. I thought it was him. I waved but the lad was asleep. Did ya not send him oot with a message ta someone?"

"No, I did not. Do ya think the woman asked him ta deliver a message to someone? If she did, why dinna she ask me and not the wee boy?" came Mr Bucket's annoyed reply.

"I dinna know, but now I think of it, I'm sure it was him. It's not often ya see a seagull dressed up in a fancy suit in a carriage around here."

"Do you know which way they went?"

"Aye. I was in the back field, Alwyn, and saw the horse and carriage go round the path at least an hour ago, up past the Cranmore Windmill. But it's a strange route to be taking, because all around there is the Howling Forest and nothing much else and then that leads ya on ta the Bonhomie Caves."

"Who was driving the horses?"

"Why, Myra Bloodvein's carriage driver, of course."

"Was she in the carriage?"

"I dinna notice. I canna be sure. Dinna worry. Maybe she sent the wee boy on an errand."

"Well, if she had she should have come and spoken to me about it, though. That's typical of the woman … thinks she owns everyone and can do what she likes. Well, I tell you, if I see her – grand woman or not – she will be getting the bad side of my tongue, and no mistake."

Stevie looked at Mr Bucket's furious face. He was glad it was her and not him who would face his wrath.

"Come on. We'll follow the route," said Mr Bucket, wiping his red forehead with his hand.

As they got back into the trap, they noticed that the air seemed salty, and sea spray hit the carriage. Mr Bucket's worried voice rang out.

"That'll be coming from them Bonhomie Caves. I hope that woman has not sent him on an errand doon there."

Chapter 10

As they approached the Howling Forest from the footpath, they could see a black carriage, but it was empty. After peering into one of the windows of the carriage, Fergal shouted out,

"Look … My hat is in there, the one I gave Stewie to wear. He must be in forest. Come on. He must be doing a job for Myra."

"Wait a minute. There's a briefcase on the side of the road. Someone must have dropped it."

"Stevie, I recognise the initials on the side of it. I think it's Mr Beavis's. What's it doing there? He was going home. Why is he here? And look … there's the stick he sometimes uses."

"Aye, something very strange is going on here," replied Mr Bucket. He then screwed up his eyes and looked up at the dense forest ahead of them.

"Well, I think we're going to find out shortly. We're going to have to go into the forest. C'mon … Let's go," said Stevie. He was walking ahead of everyone, but finding it difficult because of the moss on the covered stones and then having to make his way through wild brambles, followed by everyone else.

They entered a dark path where wide-trunked Norway spruce with finger-like branches covered in cobwebs heavily guarded the entrance. It gave off a creepy, ghostly presence, and they all nervously wondered what they were walking into.

Meanwhile, Stewie was falling in and out of a drugged blackness. At first he couldn't open his eyes. It was as if they had stuck shut. The smell of cold air was strong, and his beak detected a strong smell of pine leaves. He knew now he was somewhere outside. As he gradually came to, he groggily managed to open his sore eyes. When he tried to move, he found his wings had been fastened down with strong rope. On looking around, he saw he had been tied to the trunk of a huge tree. He lifted his chin up and gazed at his surroundings. It was a forest. A wave of fear shot through him.

What had happened to him?

He remembered Myra Bloodvein's driver appearing at Loch House while he was looking for his uncle and shouting out to him, asking if he could help him with a wheel stuck in the mud. That was all he could remember, apart from something put over his mouth as he bent down to look at the wheel. Trying to untie himself was impossible. He shouted out a weak "Help!" Then he shouted again, his voice stronger now: "Help!" He banged his body against the ropes, trying to snap them. But they were thick and tightened round him, hurting his narrow chest.

Then came another voice. It was the voice Mr Beavis.

"It is no good, whoever you are. They have made a good job of tying us to this tree. I have been trying to free myself for at least half an hour."

"What happened to me?"

Mr Beavis's weary voice replied,

"Don't you remember when you were brought you here? A thug had already waylaid my carriage. My carriage driver was in league with them. They were going to force me to act as a witness for you to sign the deeds of the house over to Myra Bloodvein. When she arrived, she went hysterical when she saw you were not Fergal. What is your name?"

"My name's Stewie. What's your name?"

"Ronald Beavis, the family solicitor of Fergal, who lives at Loch House."

"I am the nephew of Mr Bucket. Do ya think she mistook me for Fergal? He gave me some clothes, and we look a bit alike."

"Yes, I think that was what happened. At first I thought it was Fergal until I realised you were much thinner and your beaks are so different. Well, once she saw it was not him she tied us both up. What an awful woman. Do you know, she slapped me when I demanded she let me go? Even worse, she had her carriage driver tie us to this tree and said, 'Let the werewolves have a meal on him.' The evil woman then laughed. How I could have believed her to have been a lady? I am afraid we are doomed. I have heard the sounds of wolves howling. It is only a question of time before they find us.

"Oh my God. We are surely doomed," wailed the terrified solicitor.

As he spoke, Stewie gulped with fear, but then had a thought.

"I think I can get us oot of here." Stewie lifted his beak and began pecking at the rope holding him.

"What do you mean, Stewie?"

"I'm going to peck this rope."

"Of course, of course … You will use your beak. Oh, please be quick, young man. That howling is getting louder. They must be getting nearer. Please, please hurry."

Stewie did not respond. Intent on biting at the dry rope, he pecked furiously at it. The first layer came away and he continued pecking, speeding up until finally the rope broke and fell round him. Quickly, he slid out of the rope and ran down the other side of the tree to see a well-dressed gentleman stepping out of the rope and brushing himself down.

"Well done. You did it. Pleased to meet you." The solicitor shook Stewie's hand. "Now, how do we get out of this wretched place?"

"I'll guide us by flying up in the air." Stewie fluttered his wings and they felt them start to loosen up. He half-flew jerkily in the air. "That's better. A bit of cramp, but ah'll be able ta fly and see where we need to go. Dinna ya worry."

"You won't leave me, will you?"

"Of course not. Dinna worry."

Reassured, Mr Beavis gave a sigh of relief while the seagull flew high into the air and swooped back down.

"Keep ta the left. It leads on to an opening. We'll be able to walk across a grass verge from there. I'm going ta see how near it is ta the road." And with that he was back up high into the air, his wings flapping furiously.

Ronald Beavis walked tentatively, with twigs snapping underfoot. The forest was silent, but then his ears heard something almost like a sobbing.

"What on earth?" Coming into view was an old, abandoned well. The noise was coming from inside there. Peering in, he saw the red, tear-streaked face of a young girl, hanging on to the sides of a well.

"Oh, my word. Are you hurt?"

"No. Please, please, help me. I have been here all day. I can't get myself out."

"How did you end up in there?"

"I was chasing my brother and we were playing hide-and-seek. I fell in, but he must have gone back home. I have been shouting and shouting." The girl started to cry.

"Don't worry, young lady. I will get you out of there. Stewie, can you hear me?" the solicitor shouted up and looked into the air, then shouted again.

Stewie appeared above his head.

"This young lady has fallen down this well. We can't leave her. I am going to go back for the rope."

"Och, ah … See … well, be quick. The howling was awfully close and we want to get oot of here as soon as we can before it gets dark, and there's a full moon. I'll fly above your head and make sure you are going on the right route back."

"Eh, yes, I see," replied Mr Beavis, now regretting his bravado, but knowing he could not leave the girl and would have to get her out of there. "You really don't need to worry, young lady. I am going to you out of there. I won't be long." But this action only made the girl start crying again. He repeated that he would not be long and turned back.

There had been a mild rain and he could see where his shoe prints had been on some of the mud-stained grass. The rustling of the leaves on the trees made him jump once or twice and he kept looking around, half-expecting a fearsome wolf to leap on him. But, with relief, he found the tree with the rope still attached, quickly picked it up, and waved it in the air to Stewie. He raced back, as the forest appeared to be losing sunlight, and went back to the well.

"Hello," he shouted down to the girl. "I have a rope. Hold on to it and I will pull you up."

The sad-eyed girl nodded back in reply, and grabbed hold of an end of it. He pulled and he pulled, but the girl was much heavier than he expected and it took all his strength to pull her up to the surface of the well. As her face came into view he quickly helped her climb over it and on to the forest floor.

She was a strange-looking girl, with a very wide face and a yellowish complexion, which he had not noticed before, and quite big ears. As she turned her head to him, he could see slanted, light-coloured blue eyes and quite a wide mouth. Her greasy-looking black hair was tied in puppy-tail bunches and she wore a smock-like dress. He could see there were dark brown leather sandals on her thin legs.

"You are not hurt, are you?" he asked her.

"No," came the reply, which was quite toneless.

"Well, I will need to find your parents. You might as well come with me."

"No, I won't come. I live here. My family lives here."

"You live here? What is your name?"

"Rana," came the reply. And with that she gave him a strange smile, ran past him, and was gone before he realised what was happening.

"Well, of all the cheek. Not even a thank you," fumed Mr Beavis. "Did you see that, Stewie?" The solicitor looked up at the sky.

"Aye, I did. Her family must be very brave to live in a forest full of werewolves."

"I would have tried to stop her if I had known she was going to run off. Do you think I should look for her?"

"Och, it's too dark. You would get lost. The way she ran she must have known every inch of the forest. Come, we have ta get ta the road."

"Yes, I expect you are right."

"Go right past the well. Stay to your right now. It's a long path, but it will get ya oot of the forest. Best speed up, though. Ya dinna want to be in here when the moon comes oot and the water kelpies – evil little horses – are in the streams."

"Oh my God. Werewolves and kelpies? Whatever next!" Mr Beavis wiped his spectacles and half-ran down the path. But in his wake was the sound of wolves howling. This time it sounded as if every one of them was howling to the others. It was quite deafening, as if they were dangerously close.

Stewie, who was flying ahead, looked worried. There was no doubt he would be able to escape the wolves so high up in the air, but Mr Beavis was no runner. Once Stewie guided him on to the road, the man would not be safe. The concerned seagull hoped and prayed a carriage would come down the road, but it was a remote spot.

In the meantime, Bruce had sat Mrs Bucket in the rocking chair in the kitchen by a roaring fire and given her a cup of tea as he munched on a piece of warmed-up kipper. The housekeeper's hands shook as she sipped the hot tea from a bone china cup and made half the contents slide off into the saucer.

"Don't worry," said Bruce. "I'm sure he'll be fine."

There was a knock on the door and Bruce, leaving Mrs Bucket sitting by the fire, went to answer it. When he opened the door a long shadow loomed over his tiny figure, and as he looked up his big eyes saw the face of a very tall African cheetah with vivid, orange-coloured eyes. The animal was wearing a brown fedora, an ivory-coloured rubber raincoat, and black trousers. On his feet he wore black leather shoes that sparkled, they were so clean. The cheetah gave a smile, showing his dimples, and then said in a clipped British accent,

"Hello, I am Inspector Wallace Whiskerman of the Metropolitan Police. I am looking for Fergal, the nephew of Remus McFetrich. I have called on a matter of the utmost urgency."

"Hey, sorry, man. You've just missed him. Something weird has happened. The housekeeper's nephew has gone missing and Fergal's gone out with my friend and the housekeeper's husband to look for him."

"I am sorry to hear that, but I really do need to speak to him. It is most urgent. My card, you will see, shows I am from the Metropolitan Police. See here."

Bruce read the card and was suitably impressed, but then started trembling and paled at a sudden horrific thought.

"Eh … It's not anything to do with my trifle, is it?"

"Your what?"

"My trifle."

"I don't know what you're talking about. I am here on serious police business. Look, can I come in and wait? I think the weather looks like it's changing for the worse. I have travelled a long distance and I am extremely tired. The carriage driver has gone to collect my detective constables, so it will be at least an hour before he returns." The weary-eyed police inspector sighed and rubbed his furry forehead in agitation, and scratched his pristine white whiskers as he spoke.

"Of course, of course ... Hey, man, I'm so sorry. My name is Bruce. I'm a friend of Fergal's. Please come in."

The cat widened the door opening and let the cheetah in, directing him into the kitchen where it was warm. After introducing him to Mrs Bucket, he asked him to sit down at the kitchen table and he said he would make some more tea.

But, as they sat talking at the kitchen table, a large black figure loomed in the bushes outside, making grunting noises. It came closer to the house. The creature was at least six feet tall, even in its hunched state. It dripped saliva down its fangs. Coarse, black-grey hair bristled on its head. It lumbered forward. The smell of human blood made it greedy.

It lifted its pointed snout. The animal licked its lips eagerly, and its slanted blue eyes watched and listened. By following the human smell, it was led to the back of the kitchen. It was unafraid of them. It had been sent by *her*. She would reward it with the return of its skin if it killed all but some cormorant called Fergal.

As it peered in the window, its nose twitched in excitement. It lifted its great body up, and with a roar charged through the glass window. Shards of glass flew through the air, but it didn't seem to affect the werewolf. It felt no pain. The three people in the house didn't register at first what had happened. First came shock and then horror at the monstrous animal lunging towards them.

Terrified, Bruce moved Mrs Bucket away from it as it came nearer, as she began screaming.

"Come over here," hissed Wallace Whiskerman. Out of his pocket he produced a pistol and aimed it at the werewolf while continuing to hiss at it. That was when the werewolf began to roll back its head and howl. It was like the sound of the tide, almost a roar. The house shook as it howled.

"Oh my God," screamed Bruce as he dragged Mrs Bucket further away from it. Her cup and saucer and the brown liquid flew through the air and smashed into sticky pieces on the floor.

The police inspector fired his gun at its body. Instead of killing it, the blast seemed to daze it and it lay for a couple of seconds on the ground. Then, to the police inspector's horror, it started to get up again. He fired the pistol again and the bullet hit its chest, then bounced off its fur. It got up again, baring its fangs, and prepared to spring at him.

That was when Bruce, in desperation, and looking for a missile to throw at it, picked up the teapot and threw it. The teapot smashed over its head, and liquid, tea leaves, and earthenware pieces crashed to the ground as it moved forward. Bruce spied a bowl in the sink full of potato peelings, grabbed them, and threw them all across the creature's black, hairy stomach. But the creature brushed most of them off. Some of the peelings hung on to its matted fur.

The cat then threw the brown wooden salt box hanging on a hook on the wall, but aimed badly, and the salt box with the salt flying out barely touched the werewolf's fur. In desperation, Bruce spied Mrs Bucket's rock buns in an open biscuit tin and began firing them at the creature as if he was playing cricket. This time the beast went down completely, after an extremely hard one caught it on the temple. Bruce continued firing them at it until he had used the last one up.

The werewolf, stunned by the overcooked, rock-like texture of the buns, lay half-dazed on the ground. Then it crawled back up, its great height towering over him. Bruce panicked. Then he gulped and, with dismay, picked up his prize clootie dumpling. He fired the huge Christmas pudding, complete with basin, at the creature. The solid currant and mixed peel mixture dripped off the creature, and as it wiped its face an evil glint came in to its eyes.

But then something happened as it tried to get up. It fell and began howling, this time as if in pain. The coarse hair on its head began to burn. It screeched with rage, and began snapping at something imaginary in the air. Then it slowly began to slump to the floor and, with a shudder of its body, it fell to the ground as if in a deep sleep.

"What on earth? What did you do? My bullets bounced off it." As the cheetah said this, a powdery black mist began to engulf the creature and it started to change shape and shrink in size.

93

In front of them lay a figure of a man.

"Billy Plover," exclaimed Mrs Bucket. "Why, it's Jimmy Plover's laddie. He was supposed to have joined the army."

Something rattled to the ground and Wallace Whiskerman bravely went up to the man lying on the ground and picked up the object.

"Look. A silver threepenny piece, and here are another two." The cheetah turned them over and examined them carefully, and then said, "Well, Bruce, I think I know what happened. Ha ha. Never in the world could I believe something like that would happen. Of all things, a clootie dumpling. The men at the Met will never believe it when I tell them this." The cheetah kept laughing, then began holding his stomach because he had laughed so much he had made it sore.

Bruce and Mrs Bucket looked blankly at each other, thinking he had gone mad and that it was not a time to be laughing after what had happened.

"Don't you see? The silver from the threepenny piece killed the creature."

"How did that happen? The coins don't lose shape in a clootie dumping," said a puzzled Bruce.

"Eh, I think that may have been my fault. I put the clootie dumpling in the oven and it was in a wee while I looked at the recipe and realised I was supposed to have boiled it."

"Ah, Mrs Bucket, how wonderful. Well, your error may have just saved our lives. For some strange reason the coins changed shape, and became almost bullet-shaped. You must have an extremely hot oven. Well done, madam." The cheetah gave a charming smile, which made Mrs Bucket blush.

"Wow, Mrs Bucket. Am I glad you put the clootie dumpling in the oven." Bruce shook his head and went over and gave a lick on her hand, purring happily as he did. "How and why did the werewolf come here?" Bruce asked, still too frightened to go near the body on the ground.

"I am not sure, but werewolves hate silver. It's the only thing that can kill them. It's usually a silver bullet. I didn't have time to get my silver gun out of my bag. The gun was made especially for me. I certainly didn't imagine that silver threepenny pieces could do the job as well. It is a miracle. I am afraid to say that I think the creature has been sent here by someone. It might be because of me. There may be more of them. This is something we may need to prepare for. I have another two silver bullets, and that's all."

"How do you know so much about werewolves?"

The cheetah replied,

"I dealt with this type of creature a long time ago in a curious case called The Werewolf of Crouch End. Because of it and my experience I was sent here, because there have been reports of a large number of people going missing on this island. Then we heard talk of werewolves. This may seem far-fetched to people, but both I and my men have seen these creatures. One of my team came over here first, but has disappeared.

"I have brought three other constables. They have been looking for him on the Isle of Skye, but are coming over here. They might be able to provide me with some valuable information. We have a suspect who may be making the werewolves behave in this aggressive manner. It has been well known that the werewolves lived in the Howling Forest, and it is only recently that they appear to be coming out of there and attacking people.

"Someone is making them do this. We have our suspicions about who it is. That is all I can tell you at the moment."

"Och, we knew about monsters in the forest but they were doing no harm, so nobody bothered about getting rid of them. But then bad things happened and people starting going missing, and that's when people said it was the monsters doing it. A lot of my friends left the island. It was so sad ... and now this. I still canna believe Billy Plover was a werewolf," Mrs Bucket said after listening intently to the conversation the cheetah was having with Bruce.

"Yes, and unless something is done about it, things will, I am afraid to say, get worse. Bruce, did you say Mrs Bucket's nephew had gone missing?"

"Yes, Mr Bucket and my friends Stevie and Fergal have gone to look for him."

"Has a stranger been to this house recently?"

"Yes, a lady called Myra Bloodvein and her sister. We met them on our journey here and this morning she turned up at the house. She was really horrible."

"Myra Bloodvein … Was it Fergal she came to visit?"

"Yes, but she wasn't happy he had inherited the house. Would you believe she tried to buy both Fergal and me from Fergal's solicitor, Mr Beavis, for pets for her daughter?"

"I can believe anything from that lady. She could be at the root of all this. Did you say Fergal's solicitor is here?"

"Well, he was, but he's gone home now. He just needed Fergal to sign some papers."

"Ah, I see. A pity. I would like to have talked to him. There would have been a lot of people who were unhappy that your friend Fergal inherited Loch House and the land. He may be in danger."

"Fergal in danger?"

"Yes. We believe this house and land have something to do with the werewolves."

"In the cellar there is a stuffed wolf, and there are papers. I can show you. I think Mr Remus McFetrich was some sort of scientist."

"Now, that's very interesting. Yes, I think it would be a good idea if you show me the room. But first I think we will need to place this gentleman in another room. Mrs Bucket, have you a room we can place him in and a blanket to cover him? And we will need to board up the window."

"Yes. The door there on the left is the laundry room, and I can find tools and wood for the window."

Bruce and the cheetah picked up the werewolf and, directed by Mrs Bucket, carefully laid him down on the laundry stone floor. Mrs Bucket returned with a blanket and the inspector gently covered him with it. Bruce, trembling, stared fixedly at the covered figure as if half-expecting the werewolf to come back to life.

"Poor wee lad. Such a terrible thing to happen to him. He was so nice," sniffed Mrs Bucket as she gave a sign of the cross.

"How did he change into a werewolf?"

"He must have been bitten by another werewolf, Bruce," replied Wallace Whiskerman, shaking his head sadly and looking at the figure. He then stood up and said, "Right, Bruce, can you show me the cellar? Just let me get my silver gun. Mrs Bucket, I would prefer it if you came with us. We all need to stay together."

So, once Wallace had retrieved his silver gun, Bruce led the way, steadily holding a lighted lantern. Wallace lowered his head and Mrs Bucket followed behind him down the cellar steps. There was an unpleasant smell caused by the damp, a wet mushrooms type of smell. Chalky lime dust fell on their heads in lumps as they went further down the steps.

"Look, there it is," Bruce said. His voice slightly echoed as he pointed at the case with the wolf in. "And see all the paperwork on the table he was doing?"

The cheetah went over to the case and stared into it.

"My word, this is most interesting. Well, it's definitely a wolf, not a werewolf. Just extremely large," replied Wallace, as he stared at the stuffed wolf.

"Och, poor Harold. I thought he had been buried," replied Mrs Bucket.

"Harold?"

"Aye, Harold. Lovely boy, but started to go very strange. We couldn't handle him any longer. He went for people. Alwyn had to shoot him because he leapt on the master and went for his throat, and the day before he had gone for me. Very sad affair. He had never done anything like that before. Aye, it was very sad. Alwyn was fair upset."

Wallace gave a sympathetic nod, but was distracted by a small grey journal he had found in some loose papers on the desk. As he went through it he bent forward, and carefully looked through the diagrams and handwritten notes on loose pages. Finally he found a page, which he returned to and reread.

"That's it. I've found it," he said excitedly, and turned more pages. His sharp eyes missed nothing. "I hoped we would find something like this."

"Like what?" Bruce craned his neck, but was too short to see over Wallace's shoulder as he was so much taller than him.

"This is what we should have been looking for … All this time we have spent with our investigations. So the poor man wasn't in league with the werewolves, and never was. Remus McFetrich wasn't helping them. Now I understand what he was trying to do. He was trying to find a cure to stop people turning into werewolves. Trying to do that would have made certain people angry … And see, he mentions something about werewolf skins. I wonder what he means."

As he patted his whiskered chin, Wallace Whiskerman turned more pages, eagerly reading them and scratching the pages with his long claws.

"Mrs Bucket, do you know what Mr McFetrich died of?"

"No, sir. He had a choking fit and had to go to his bed. He never recovered, and died a few days later."

"I see. Did anyone come to visit him during that period?"

"Oh, aye."

"Did Myra Bloodvein visit him?"

"Aye, she did, sir. Brought him a game pie, but he could only eat a wee bit. I didna like the look of it. It smelt funny, and I threw the rest oot."

"Hmm … I see," came the cheetah's reply, and he narrowed his deep-set orange eyes.

"Mr Whiskerman, there are some outhouses outside. There are some very large skeletons in there. Do you think they could be werewolves?"

"Oh, are there? I don't know, Bruce. We'll have to check it. Mr McFetrich did keep a large number of wild animals, from what I have heard. But please do not call me Mr Whiskerman. Call me Wallace."

"Sure. Will do, Wallace. Mrs Bucket said Godric the lion had been poisoned. Isn't that right, Mrs Bucket?"

"Aye. He was. The wee pussy is speaking the truth. I know a poisoned animal when I see one, and dinna take any notice of what Myra Bloodvein said. I am telling you that lion was poisoned."

"Was Myra around the time the lion was poisoned?"

"Aye. She brought over some fruit cake. I dinna know why she kept calling on Master McFetrich. He did not like her at all."

"Do you think Myra poisoned the lion and Mr McFetrich?" asked Bruce, shocked.

"It's a possibility."

"Are you saying that woman poisoned my master and Godric?" burst out Mrs Bucket angrily.

"Well, we can't say for sure yet," came Wallace's careful reply, as he placed the journal in his coat pocket and patted it down with one of his paws.

Bruce, horrified, could only stare at the cheetah. His first thought was,

How would Fergal take that news?

As if reading his thoughts, the cheetah looked at him and said,

"I am not going to say any more on the matter. We need to get back upstairs and wait for my men."

Abruptly, he stood up and made to go up the cellar steps. Mrs Bucket and Bruce then followed the cheetah back upstairs, at the same time as giving each other troubled looks. The first thing Wallace then did was to board all the doors up with wood, with Bruce helping him as he went to each window with Mr Bucket's hammer and nails. Once this job was done, he gave strict instructions.

"No one now goes outside, understand? We don't want anyone else going missing."

Bruce and Mrs Bucket nodded back in reply.

"Right. My men will be here shortly. I am going to make sure I have some silver bullets left. Mrs Bucket, get together any guns your master may have had, and any other weapons."

"Yes, sir."

The cheetah looked at Mrs Bucket and Bruce. He was trying not to look worried in front of them but he knew that Bruce and Mrs Bucket would be no match if there was another attack, and this time by a pack of werewolves. He was the only one with silver bullets. Myra Bloodvein could arrive any time with her henchmen and the werewolves before his men got there. She would be after Fergal. He hoped and prayed his men arrived before them. They would all be armed with silver bullets.

After guiding everyone inside he bolted the front door.

Chapter 11

Myra Bloodvein was not happy. Her useless carriage driver had picked up the wrong bird.

"How could you get it wrong, you fool?" she screamed hysterically at the carriage driver as she hit him across the face with her jewelled hand and made a red mark on his face. While trying to duck the blows he kept his head down as she continued to swipe at him. He was a big, beefy-looking man, with tufts of black, wiry hair sticking up on his head. A simple man, she had taken him on because of his size and the fact that all she had to do was have him act as a thug for her.

"I have had to send one of the werewolves out to get the bird. Why has he not reported back? He should have been back by now."

There was no answer from the carriage driver. He was now at the side of the road, rubbing his head. Myra climbed back into her crested black coach and tutted to herself. Then she shouted out to the carriage driver as he climbed back into the driver's seat.

"Take me back to Loch House. If that werewolf has eaten the bird, it may not be a problem. I can get the bird's signature forged. At least I have that solicitor's signature, so that's something, but it will be a shame about the cat if it has been eaten. My daughter wanted it as a pet. Still, at least I don't have to concern myself with that solicitor. I should think the werewolves have had him and the other bird as a snack by now." She smiled, amused at the thought of the pompous solicitor being eaten. "Come on. Move on, fool. Do something right today," she hissed as she hummed a strange tune.

The nervous carriage driver took the reins and the coal-black horses travelled with full speed back to Loch House.

Mr Beavis was desperate to get away from the forest. He felt like he had walked miles, when in fact he had only walked a short distance. It was creepy. Dark shadows seemed to follow him as he walked. Distorted trees looked like hunchbacked witches with long, pointed fingernails, and he found himself continually looking at them to make sure they were just trees and not moving towards him. There was an unpleasant damp smell, and pools of old rainwater dripped off the bushes, making strange whistling noises as he passed them.

The forest was barren. No flowers were growing there. Everything seemed to be dying or in a state of decay. He was tickled by hanging moss and spiderwebs as he walked further, and they made him brush against damp leaves. A half-eaten dead mouse lay in his path.

"Ugh … Horrible, horrible place," he muttered as he jumped over it and twisted his mouth in disgust. He watched carefully for kelpies as he crossed the stream, but there were none. Then finally, to his relief, he saw the clearing. Sitting on a dark brown fencepost was Stewie, waving at him with a broad grin.

"I think I recognise some of this place. Ma uncle took me here once a long time ago. We need to walk up that hill. I'll fly up ahead and see if there's a carriage going by. If not, there will be a long walk and a long flight home. Keep ya fingers crossed there is a carriage on the road."

"Oh, I do hope so."

The bird then flew off again.

Although he was puffing and panting up the hill, the solicitor struggled on. His clothes were soaking wet with sweat and his shoes, which were not built for walking, felt very uncomfortable. When he looked up at the sky he could see the outline of Stewie. The bird then seemed to turn his body around in mid-air. His wings then started beating erratically as he flew towards Mr Beavis.

"I've seen them. I've seen them. They're here," the excited bird shouted breathlessly.

"Who?"

"Ma uncle, Stevie, and Fergal. They have the trap. They must have been looking for me. I'm going back to make sure they see us. Once ya get over the top of the hill, you will see the horse and cart."

"Thank heavens for that. I didn't like the idea of a long walk back to Loch House," came the relieved reply.

The bird flew off.

101

One last stagger up the hill and the solicitor came to the top of it. He could see the horse and cart but no sign of anyone else, until he heard a rustle of the bushes and worriedly looked across at them. But that look was taken over by recognition. Stevie, Fergal, Mr Bucket, and Stewie came through them.

Stewie told them what had happened to both himself and Mr Beavis.

A concerned Mr Bucket listened carefully and said,

"We need ta get back to the house. My wife and Bruce will not be safe. That woman, Myra Bloodvein, will be looking for you, Fergal, to get you ta sign the will."

"Yes, he's right. Come on, everyone. We have to get back," replied Stevie, answering for Fergal, who appeared to be still thinking about what Mr Bucket had said. Both Stevie and Fergal were worrying about Bruce as well as Mrs Bucket.

Everyone piled back into the horse and trap. Mr Bucket made clicking noises to the horse and the animal took off. He raised the reins to make the horse go faster. The animal raced round bends, but this only resulted in everyone collapsing on top of one another in the carriage.

They arrived back at the house in record time, but Myra's carriage was not outside. Mr Bucket leapt down and, shouting his wife's name, hammered on the front door. The door opened a crack and a large yellow cat peered out.

"Who are you? Ya'd better not have harmed my wife. You'd betta not have, cos I'll break ya neck if ya have."

"Calm down. I am Inspector Walter Whiskerman from the London Met. I am investigating the disappearance of a Percival Pranworthy, who was last seen on this island," came the annoyed reply. This was followed by a long yawn from the cheetah. It had been a long day.

"Och … Sorry," replied Mr Bucket, reddening with embarrassment.

"Aye, calm down, ya daft beggar," came the voice of Mrs Bucket as she pushed past the inspector and hugged her husband and Stewie.

Behind, the tiny figure of Bruce peered out under the armpit of Mr Whiskerman.

"Ya wouldnae believe what's happened. We had a werewolf, of all things, in the house. Can ya believe it? But we fettled him with the help of some of my baking, didn't we, lads?" Mrs Bucket looked back at the cheetah and Bruce and gave a short laugh.

"We certainly did, Mrs Bucket," the cheetah answered, displaying his brilliant white teeth as he smiled. "But where have you been? I believe Stewie went missing," the cheetah said, wrongly looking at Fergal.

"No, I am Fergal. This is Stewie."

Just as Stewie was about to speak, Mr Beavis gave a slight cough and then butted in. He told them what had happened and when he had finished, the inspector said,

"Well, they will be after Fergal, that I am in no doubt of. Myra wants this property for some reason and needs him to sign it over to her. Fergal, stay with everyone and do not go off on your own. Is that understood?"

The cormorant meekly answered "Yes," to the inspector's strong voice of authority.

"Now, who are you?" The cheetah looked at Stevie as he spoke.

"Stevie Rump, sir."

"Ah, yes. Your parents are setting up an orphanage in Edinburgh, I believe."

"How did you know that?"

"Ah, I know a lot of things. We had to investigate Fergal and any friends he had after Percival Pranworthy disappeared. He is fifteenth in line to the throne. We believe he was killed because of his position in the line of succession, and there is a plot to remove other members of the royal family. Some of them have already gone missing. There have been many assassination attempts on Queen Victoria." The cheetah absent-mindedly pulled on one of his whispers as he spoke.

"Percival was fifteenth in line to the throne of England?" exclaimed Mr Beavis in amazement.

"Yes, he was. We have an idea who is behind this and that's why my investigations led me here, but first I think we should all get in the house. I am waiting for my team and I am hoping they arrive before Myra and whatever she has brought with her. I will open the door if there is a knock. No one else answers it but me. Understood?"

Everyone said "Yes," to the cheetah. His serious face showed he meant business.

"Mr Bucket, we have, as you can see, boarded up the windows. Can you check them for me? If Myra comes, she might bring more werewolves with her."

Mrs Bucket gave a shrill scream when the word 'werewolf' was mentioned, causing her husband to place a comforting arm around her.

"Dinna worry yourself. It'll be all right." He didn't sound convincing, and she continued to cry. After giving her one last hug he went to check the windows were secure, leaving Bruce to comfort her further.

Myra was in a rage. Screeching, she stamped her foot. She was at Joe Plump's farm, and heading back to Loch House.

"Where is he?"

That bird was not at Loch House. Hadn't that thick farmer said Fergal had gone out in the horse and carriage to look for the seagull? He must be along the road, she thought, scratching her chin, which had warts embedded into it.

She turned to the carriage driver and barked,

"Find him, idiot, and bring him to me. Look for carriage tracks. Do I have to think of everything?"

The gorilla-like driver, his head down at being shouted at, scratched his armpits and grunted, and got out of the carriage. He then proceeded to look along the grass verge and then went back into the forest, glad to be away from her.

Myra fumed to herself. How the carriage driver could have mistaken a seagull for a cormorant was unbelievable. Stupid, ignorant man. She would sort the carriage driver out later, but first he had to get that scrawny bird and get him to sign the will. And, well, at least the solicitor was now out of the way.

Not that she had any fear of the werewolves herself. In fact, they were frightened of her. She had the power to control them. She had their werewolf souls kept in a very secret place. The Sand Witches kept them hidden for her. She had been left a book by one of her relatives. It was an ancient black magic book. It had given her the power she had craved to have full control over the beasts. The werewolves would never find their souls and because of that they were doomed to serve her, or she would set their wolfskins ablaze and they would be burnt to death.

Happy now that the windows were securely boarded, Mr Bucket felt relieved. Wallace then had a great idea. He hammered pieces of silver from the coins from the pudding into the wood and gave a smile of satisfaction as he admired his handiwork.

"I just hope this works. They are hardly silver bullets."

"Aye, well, we'll just have ta see," replied Mr Bucket sombrely.

"Come on. Let's go inside." But the sound of horses' hooves galloping up to Loch House stopped them in their tracks. Wallace, after touching the pistol in his breast pocket with one of his paws, looked up, but then relaxed when he realised the carriage held some of his men – a hyena and two humans.

"Gentlemen, am I pleased to see you!" The carriage door opened and a spiky-haired spotted hyena stepped out, who was dressed in a baggy, light blue jumper and dirty, chocolate-brown trousers that smelt of fish. He was followed by a very tall, young-looking human called Miles. Miles was blue-eyed, with a very white face. His straight brown hair was worn in a middle parting.

"Ugh. You stink, Henrik."

"Sorry, sir, but I have been undercover. And I thought that if I were a fisherman I would get to find out a lot of information about her."

"Eh? Oh, well done. Good man. I see, and what have you discovered? This chap, by the way, is Mr Bucket. He is the housekeeper's husband."

The police constable nodded back at Mr Bucket and said "Hello." He was half-smiling and unnaturally displaying long, conical bone-crushing teeth.

"It's worse than we thought, sir. There are more parties involved." After looking at Mr Bucket the hyena went silent.

"It is fine, Henrik. You can talk in front of him. He won't know what you are talking about."

Mr Bucket pursed his lips, raised his eyebrows, and went inside, but not before giving the hyena a frosty look. Bruce peeped through the door and stared at the brown-faced hyena, but stayed well inside in case he needed to run. He could not understand what breed of dog the hyena was. He seemed to have a thick neck and forequarters, but underdeveloped hindquarters. His head was wide and flat, with a blunt muzzle. His spotted ears, which were quite rounded and covered in saffron, covered the reddish-brown spots on top of his fur. He stood hunched forward as he spoke to the inspector.

"What is that?" Bruce whispered to Stevie, who was behind him.

"He's a hyena. African, I think. I'm sure I read about them in a textbook. Do you know they can crush bones and are as strong as lions?"

"I hope he keeps away from me. Looks like some sort of horrible dog to me."

"He is a policeman. You want him near you, the way things are going. Sounds like there is going to be a lot of trouble."

"Hmm," Bruce replied stiffly. He had no intention of going anywhere near the strange doglike animal.

Chapter 12

The cheetah, the hyena, and the human policeman called Miles were talking intently, and Bruce and Stevie were listening into their conversation.

"Myra, sir, has been involved in the dark arts and also with a warlock called Mordeith. A nasty piece of work," said Miles.

"Mordeith, you say? I had hoped I would never hear that name mentioned again. He disappeared five years ago and now seems to have resurfaced. He was responsible for all the kidnappings of children of wealthy parents. The families paid a fortune to get their children back. We never caught him. We knew he had gone underground somewhere, and no doubt changed his appearance. Oh, yes, I know him well. Yes, and he is as evil as her." The cheetah gave a low growl as he spoke.

"Sir," ventured Henrik, "we have another problem. Myra Bloodvein appears to have found a way of controlling the werewolves. They obey her every word. Until she came to the island the werewolves, I have been told, kept to themselves. One of the locals, who did not wish to be named, said Myra was trying to take over the whole of Howly Island. The locals have been threatened by her thugs."

Until this point the hyena had sounded very serious, but in mid-sentence he proceeded to give soft grunt-laughs, which ended in a maniacal full laugh.

"Henrik ..." said the cheetah, but he knew when the hyena started to laugh he would have to finish it. Henrik had told him he couldn't help it, and everyone in his family appeared to have this strange affliction. Even at funerals, at least one family member would embarrassingly give a 'who-oop' call, followed by lunatic laughing. Suffice to say, Henrik was not invited to many funerals.

Finally the hyena finished laughing and Wallace said, after giving a small sigh and raising his eyes upwards to heaven, asked,

"Finished?"

"Er, yes, sir."

"Good."

"Sir, but there is good news. We have an informant. Look."

Standing by the carriage was a black-haired, swarthy-skinned man with a barrel belly. He was heavy-browed and clad in ripped overalls, and he looked with distrust at the hyena as the animal spoke.

"This is William Buck. He has promised to tell us all he knows about Myra Bloodvein, but only on condition that he is given a safe passage to Australia for both himself and his family."

"I see. Well, Mr Buck, if we find the information useful, yes, we will do this. You will find I always keep my promises. However, if I find you have told me a pack of lies, you would not want me as an adversary." The orange-eyed cheetah bent forward and looked directly into the informant's eyes in an intimidating manner until William Buck had to look away from the cold, penetrating gaze.

"Oh, I have a lot ta tell you. But what I tell ye will make me and ma family in danger. She will have us killed, I tell ya. The woman is in league with the devil, ah tell ya." His insolent expression changed and the man now looked very frightened, and used a dirty finger to wipe a thin line of sweat on his unshaven lip.

"Tell us what you know, Mr Buck." The cheetah's tone was now gentle, as he could see the man was shaking with fright.

"Myra moved ta the Isle of Skye a couple of years ago. I was told she needed men to help her with people who were causing her bother. Well, ya know, I'm handy with my fists. I may be small, but I can easy fell a man." As if to exaggerate this point, William Buck rolled his fists into balls and made a pretend punch in the air towards the inspector. Then he continued, saying,

"The first job ah had ta do was go to Mulliver's Solicitors and tell Mr Machran he had ta give me his files on a list ah'd been given by her. At first he wasn't obliging, but after a few words with him he gave me the files. Ah feel bad about that. The man was terrified, but ah had to feed and clothe my family." The man looked ruefully at the cheetah.

"Go on," came the abrupt reply.

"Well, that list … I have a good memory, see, and when I give the files to her ah remembered all the names on there. See, it's all in ma head, and ah can give ya every one of them names."

"Why would the list be so important to us?"

"Because I recognised the names on the list. Most of them were in the royal family. One was the Earl of Pembrokeshire. He's an important man, that ah know."

"I see. Well, yes, we will give you and your family safe passage to Australia. You will need to tell us all the names on the list. I think we should go in to discuss this matter further. I do know of the Earl of Pembrokeshire. He is currently on our missing persons files."

"Ya will have to write you will do this fa me, that ya will protect me and my family if Myra goes ta prison. I need something ya have written ta say this."

"Of course, of course, man. Come on inside. I don't like conducting business outside."

Wallace Whiskerman beckoned Henrik and Miles to come inside with them and introduced them to everyone else, then told Miles to check the premises were secure. The inspector guided William Buck into the library, along with Henrik, and ushered Mr Beavis also to come inside. He then closed the door firmly behind him on Stevie, Fergal, Bruce, and Stewie just as they tried to go in.

"I don't think he wanted us in there, did he?"

"No, I don't think he did," replied Fergal, scrunching up his scarred beak.

"C'mon, let's go into the kitchen," said Bruce, on noticing Mr Bucket had gone into the kitchen. They did as he said.

With Miles the detective constable going through the house and making sure everything was blocked up, Bruce sat at the kitchen table and reached for the biscuit tin, which contained rounds of his home-made currant shortbread. He handed some out to everyone. Mrs Bucket then set the kettle on the stove to make a pot of tea. Bruce was carefully placing precious tea leaves from the tea chest into the teapot when he looked up at the cellar door.

"Guys, I think we should go back down there. We might find something that Mr Whiskerman will find useful."

"Well, I think you're right, but you know it's like trouble follows us, what with the Island of Glendowwer. My mum and dad will go spare when they find out what's been happening."

"Well, it's not your fault. I'm just glad you guys came here with me."

Stevie gave Fergal a rueful smile in response to this and flattened his hair, which was sticking up at a peculiar angle on one side, with one of his hands.

"Fergal, we just have to make sure you're safe from that horrible woman. Look what she did to Stewie."

"I know. I'm terrified of her."

"Don't worry. We'll keep you safe," said Bruce comfortingly, as he placed a striped paw on one of Fergal's hand feathers.

"Dinna worry. The police are here. You'll be fine," said Mr Bucket, who was feeling sorry for the forlorn-looking cormorant as he shook his head sadly.

"Yes, but it's all my fault … what happened to Stewie and Mr Beavis."

The voice of Mrs Bucket broke in. She was feeling sorry for the sad-eyed bird, who was clucking to himself.

"Dinna fret yourself, laddie. Wee Stewie is fine. Does he look like he's suffering now?" Fergal lifted his head and looked at Stewie, who had his beak covered in shortbread crumbs as he happily bit into biscuit after biscuit in the tin.

"No, I s'pose he doesn't," he said, instantly cheering up.

"Come on, Bruce. You wanted to go down the cellar, didn't you? We can have a cup of tea when we come back up," said Stevie, swiftly changing the subject.

"Oh, yes, come. Let's have one last look. You never know; we might find something."

Stewie finished his biscuit and joined Fergal and Stevie as they made their way to the cellar. Bruce turned around and smiled at Mrs Bucket, then noticed that she was filling a huge china soup bowl with milk.

"What's that for?" he asked, curiously cocking his head.

"Oh, eh … I use it to get stains out of my washing," came the reply.

"Do you? And it gets rid of stains? I've never heard of that before."

"Bruce, come on," came Stevie's impatient reply.

"Oh, eh … sorry. Coming." Bruce followed swiftly behind, closing the cellar on his way down.

Mr Bucket looked at his wife after he had gone.

"That was a close one. Ya're going ta have to tell him."

"I know, I know, but in my own good time," came the worried reply.

Chapter 13

Bruce was still thinking about the remedy for removing stains with milk when he shuffled down the cellar steps with Stevie. That was until he found himself flying high into the air. His yell made Stevie turn around, but he caught him just in time as he was about to fall down the steps.

As Stevie clutched hold of him and gently placed him down, to the gasping thanks of the tabby cat, he said,

"You all right?"

"Yeah, yeah. Thanks, man. Thought I was going to be a goner."

"Sure you're all right?" asked another voice – Fergal's.

"Yep, sure. I should have looked where I was going," came the muted reply. Bruce was now getting a bit embarrassed with all the attention.

It was then that Stevie noticed that he had displaced a ragged piece of red carpet with his foot at the base of the cellar steps. When he moved his foot, he could now see what was underneath. It was a wooden trapdoor.

"Hey, guys, look at this," he shouted excitedly.

"Wow … Look at that."

Stevie pulled at a rusty ring on the trap door with Fergal, Stevie, and Bruce helping him. It was difficult at first, but they pulled and pulled, and finally it grudgingly opened with a screechy, bone-crunching creak. As they peered into the darkness Bruce handed Stevie a lantern. They could see narrow limestone steps going down into the darkness.

"I'm going to go down the steps and see what's there. Hey, look … There are no cobwebs on the trapdoor. Maybe someone has been down here before. If I take the lantern first, get another one from upstairs before I go down."

"I'll come with you," replied Fergal.

"Bruce, go and get another lantern," said Stevie.

Bruce didn't need to be asked twice, and raced upstairs to ask Mrs Bucket for a lantern. The idea of being in the dark in a cellar was not something he relished. He might be a cat and his eyes could see in the dark better than any of the others, but this cellar was quite spooky and, what with a stuffed wolf in a cage, it gave him the willies. He also didn't fancy going down the trapdoor steps. The other thing Bruce didn't like to admit, especially with him being a cat, was that he was afraid of the dark.

Once Stevie was handed the lantern, he went gingerly down the cellar steps, his lanky body walking with difficulty. His large feet hung over the narrow cellar steps. At the bottom of the steps was a door. He shouted up and said,

"I'm going to go through there and see what's there."

"I'm coming down with you," said Fergal, and he caught hold of a second lantern and flew down before Stevie could answer. Stewie, his wings outstretched, followed him. He did not want to miss anything.

"I'll wait here in case the trapdoor shuts up on you," said Bruce.

"OK."

After opening the door, which was lower than his height, Stevie moved his head downwards to crouch down and went through with Fergal. Stewie, who had now carefully landed on the ground, followed him. Ahead of them appeared to be a labyrinth of passageways, but which one should they take? The narrow passageway smelt strangely of coal dust and the ground was covered in sharp-edged pieces of coal, which were embedded into it and made it look like patterned flooring. Stevie lifted the lantern high and could see there was a line of archways with unlit candles. He quickly lit a few of them as he walked to give more light.

"This is so creepy," whispered Stewie, but as he said it his voice echoed around them and they all jumped.

"I know. I hope we find a way out of here. Don't you think we should mark where we walk just in case we get lost?"

"What with Stewie?"

"I can use my beak to scratch long lines on the walls, so we can recognise them if we have to come back."

"But, Fergal, we can fly up in the air," Stewie answered back.

"I know, but just in case we get lost."

"Fergal, can you hear something?"

"Yes. I think it sounds like running water."

"Aye, I can hear it now. I can hear it now. It's more like a buzzing."

When they came round the corner they could now see it. It was a small waterfall, but the ground was slippery. They put down their lanterns and just stared in awe.

"That canna be under ya uncle's house."

"No, I think it must be a passageway leading to a beach. We must be way past the house by now. How weird. I wonder if Mrs Bucket knows about it." They were sprayed with water as they came closer to it, and the smell of sea salt was now very strong in their nostrils.

"Look, can you see there? Look, stepping stones ... and see there behind it? Look ... Look." Fergal was so excited that he half-flew up in the air and beat his wings and squawked as he spoke, so much that he nearly tripped over one of his webbed feet. But Stevie grabbed his feathered arm quickly to steady him.

"Wow it's a door behind the waterfall," answered Stevie, as he stared fascinated at the blue, white-flowing curtain of water pouring downwards.

Stevie went first, his feet half-sliding over the slippery stepping stones. As he wobbled he grabbed at the door and went through it. Fergal and Stewie had no problem. They just swam through the water.

As Stevie opened the door with the others behind him they just stared, transfixed. Facing them was a narrow beach, but it seemed to be lit by the moonlight only. It was as if the sky had been covered in thick, black blankets, through which clouds had desperately tried to poke their faces. Prehistoric-looking granite rocks led the way down to the black, grimy beach. Twisted black tree roots seemed to grow out of the sand at awkward angles, casting ghostlike shadows.

"Where are we?"

"Stevie, I think I know where we are and ah hope I'm wrong," replied Stewie, his voice shaking with fear.

"Where?"

114

"I think it's the black caves. It's not a good place ta be, from what I've heard. And even worse, the Fee Sisters – the Mermaids of the Black Sea – live here." Stewie started to stutter and tremble as he spoke.

"Oh, yes. I heard about them. I'm not sure if we should go any further," replied an equally worried Stevie.

"Oh, come on. We've come this far. Let's see what's here. We won't go far, and we'll get back behind the waterfall if there's trouble. Anyway, I don't see any mermaids, do you?" was Fergal's petulant reply.

"Och, you haven't heard what I have about them. Ah think ah will go back, guys. They are ghost mermaids. They eat anything, from what I have heard, and I mean anything." replied Stewie. This terrified them.

But as he spoke there was a deafening noise. The sand seemed to open under him and then came like what sounded like singing, but not something you would ever have heard before. It was unearthly, and went into high-pitched banshee-like shrieks that echoed around them.

Stewie, Fergal, and Stevie put their hands over their heads to block out the sound. Then the repetitive din changed to a dull, single note that went through their whole bodies.

"I think I'm going to fall," said Fergal, as he slid to the ground in a deep faint. The sand seemed to gather around him in a thick, lumpy blanket. Stevie then saw what it was. Long, black fingers with misshapen claws came out of the ground and started to drag him along the ground. Stevie grabbed at Fergal and then, as he looked at Stewie, he saw he was also starting to fall, and his eyes were closed.

"Guys, wake up," shouted Stevie, but his eyelids started to close as he tried to stay awake. As he did he could feel his feet sinking into the sand as a bony hand gripped him. As he felt his strength go, he too started to get sucked into the black sand that smelt of coal.

Chapter 14

Wallace Whiskerman could not settle. He had not wanted to get too comfortable. He sat in a wonky rocking chair in the library and talked to Mr Beavis. Every now and again he would stretch his neck to look out of the window, while balancing his teacup on his lap.

He could not imagine a woman like Myra Bloodvein giving up so easily. He felt in his bones that she would come. After all, didn't the woman need Fergal to sign Loch House over to her? Mr Beavis mopped his brow in an agitated state with his handkerchief. A wash in the china basin in his bedroom had made him feel reasonably clean, but there was no time for a hot bath, which he would have liked to have had.

"I just want to go home," the solicitor kept repeating to Wallace.

"But, Ronald, you would not be safe to leave this house. We are keeping you here for your own protection and we have sent the carriage driver away to get more men," the cheetah repeated for the third time, now getting bored with having to repeat himself.

"But why do you need more men?"

"Because I think we will have to prepare for a war," responded Wallace, with no hint of emotion.

"Oh, dear God."

"Yes, I am afraid so."

"But I do not know how to fight."

"Do not worry. We are here to protect you. The men will have loaded their silver bullets. They will come prepared."

"Oh my God. Whatever possessed me to come to this wretched place?" the solicitor said in reply as he shook his head and tried to block a horrifying image of werewolves in his mind.

"Well, of course, we might not need them. It's just in case Myra brings followers here."

As Wallace spoke, the coal fire in the library went out and black smoke came into the room. Then, it started – an icy, howling wind, which made the teacups rattle. The noise became louder and the china vase on the windowsill wobbled unsteadily.

"That wind is terrible."

Wallace lifted his head, sniffed the air, and gave a low growl as he realised what it was. He recognised the scent he had picked up.

"I do not think it's the wind, Mr Beavis. Miles, make sure you are armed. I think we are about to get a visitor. Take Mrs Bucket and Mr Beavis into the cellar with Bruce and Fergal. Tell them to lock themselves in."

Then came a clatter of horses' hooves outside. Mr Beavis and Henrik went to look out of the window. Myra Bloodvein's shiny, crested black carriage had arrived. Following it were gigantic shapes, which became clearer. They were grey and black werewolves.

Noticing a horrified Ronald Beavis peering out of the window, Myra raised her eyebrows in surprise, then looked at his companion, Wallace Whiskerman. The look showed no warmth. She pulled a wry face and climbed out of the carriage. She held the hem of her dress as she walked up to the door, and her burly carriage driver accompanied her.

Next to the carriage two werewolves, with hunchbacks and spiked hair on end, lay down, awaiting her instructions. Their grisly heads were three times the size of a human's. One of them licked its huge paws, displaying yellow, pointed teeth. If it had been standing it would have been at least six feet in height – not as tall as Wallace Whiskerman, but its barrel chest was twice the size of the cheetah's.

"Hello," shouted Myra as she walked over, wearing a black dress and a grey bonnet with a bone hairpin stuck in the side of it. Tendrils of black hair fell down her face as she tapped impatiently on the ground with her cobra-headed walking stick, and she came up to the door as Wallace opened it. "I do not believe we have met."

"I am Inspector Wallace Whiskerman of the Metropolitan Police," came the silky voice.

"Ah, a policeman *and* a cheetah. How very interesting. I am Myra Bloodvein and, as you can see, I have brought two of my lovely companions." She spat out the words contemptuously, and gave a twisted smile as she said this.

"Charmed."

"We have come to see Fergal."

"He does not wish to see you."

"How do you know? You have not asked him."

"I am dealing with all his affairs now."

"Are you, indeed? Well, you are a very stupid policeman. You could save yourself and anyone else in the house if you let us have him."

"No, I don't think so."

"Do you know werewolves are very interesting creatures? They can crush the bones of their prey. It is a very horrible way to die. Isn't that right, Gargon?"

The werewolf to her right looked at her and stood up on its haunches, showing its full, lumbering height. Catching sight of a thin tree, it went over to it and ripped it out of the ground with its teeth. Then, smirking, it threw the uprooted tree to one side.

"See what he can do? Imagine what he could do to a human. He especially likes to kill humans very slowly, don't you, Gargon? He could break a scrawny cheetah's neck with one paw." She laughed cruelly as she spoke.

The werewolf grinned evilly back at her and nodded, and a crazed look came into its red eyes as it listened to her.

"As I have said, Fergal does not wish to speak to you, madam."

"Enough of this nonsense … I warned you. Gargon, this gentleman is being rude to me. Can you deal with him?" Myra moved aside as the huge creature stood up and charged at Wallace.

But, in that split second, Wallace had removed his pistol from his coat pocket and fired at the creature. At first the beast continued to move, but there followed a second shot from his pistol with one of its silver bullets and the werewolf fell shakily to the ground. A thick mist slowly gathered around it.

"Bane!" screamed Myra as the second werewolf sprang up and charged at Wallace. But, as he went to fire his pistol, the bullet stuck fast and the gun didn't fire. The creature rolled on top of him and knocked him to the ground. Its jaws snapped at him, and he wrestled with it and tried to keep it away from his throat.

But then the creature seemed to look and attack the air with its paws as it howled with rage. It was fighting something, and saliva dripped off its chin as it charged at the empty air. But there was nothing in front of it.

A shot fired above Wallace's head and he looked up to see Henrik crouched forward, firing a second time at the creature. The bullet hit its forehead and the animal sank into the ground and rolled back on top of Wallace, its dying breath on Wallace's neck. While pulling himself out of the dead animal's embrace he struggled with the sheer weight of it. As he jerkily stood up, he could have sworn he heard a lion's roar.

He shook his head and shakily stood up, then heard feet running. It was Myra racing back into her carriage. As the carriage driver rode away with her he could hear her shouting commands to him.

"Get her," he shouted to Henrik, but he was too late. The carriage driver had raced off, with the huge wheels of the carriage screeching as they rolled forward.

As they ran to their carriage, Wallace shouted to Miles, who still had his pistol raised at the entrance of the door as he anxiously looked around,

"Stay on guard here. Make sure nothing – and I mean nothing – gets in the house. We'll go after Myra."

"Yes, sir," replied Miles, who was well over six feet five. He placed his pistol back in his breast pocket.

Then Wallace and Henrik raced into the carriage and slammed the door behind them as the carriage driver made clicking noises to move the horse along.

Chapter 15

Bruce, hearing the commotion as he came out of the cellar, charged to the front door with Mr and Mrs Bucket and Mr Beavis. The two werewolves were changing, and were now two humans. The monster-like mist around them had now started to clear.

"See that? The Barham brothers. Not nice lads, but you wouldna wish such a horrible thing ta hev happened to the poor wee souls," said Mrs Bucket in reply to Mr Beavis before he spoke.

"We'll move them, sir," replied Miles.

"Ah have a place we can put them, along with the other one."

The policeman and Mr Bucket removed the now still figures and took them inside. Bruce could only stare at the commotion. His neck was sore where he had constantly turned his head to see what everyone was doing. As he went to go inside he felt a hot tongue lick his face. The feeling was strangely comforting, and he almost forgot where he was until he opened his eyes and looked around.

Facing him was an enormous golden lion with a halo-like glow around its face and body. It sat in front of him and moved one of its paws towards him. Bruce leapt in the air in fright and made to run away, but was stopped by Mrs Bucket.

"Calm yourself, laddie. It's only Godric. He wouldna harm a fly, would you, laddie?"

The golden-eyed lion turned to Mrs Bucket and looked almost lovingly into her eyes.

"No," he roared, making a breeze as he spoke.

"Aah … Help," shouted a hysterical Bruce. He was almost wetting himself.

"Laddie, he's gentle as a lamb."

Godric, smelling Bruce's fear, touched him gently with his great paw and stroked the top of the trembling cat's head gently, but it was like being cuffed about the head. This only made the little cat become paralysed with fear.

"Nice boy," whispered Bruce. His heart was racing, and it felt as if his heart was in his mouth. But the lion continued to stroke him, this time with a lighter touch of his vast paw.

"He just wants to be friends, laddie."

"Eh, yes, I see he does now," Bruce replied, half-relaxing as the lion now yawned and rolled on its back.

"Tickle his tummy. He likes that."

Bruce nervously did as Mrs Bucket said and started to laugh as he watched Godric stretch and start purring, almost like a normal moggy. Why, almost like him.

"The milk in the soup bowl was for him, wasn't it?" asked Bruce.

"Aye, it was. He loves his milk."

"If he's dead, why is he still here, Mrs Bucket?"

"He doesn't want to go into the light. Godric wants to stay with us. My lovely boy wants to just be with us. Poor wee soul." Mrs Bucket took out her handkerchief as she spoke, and tears fell down her face. "The master was so happy when he came back to us. It was as if he had never gone."

"Where does he sleep?"

"Well, he would like to sleep in your room again. He would be no bother. He misses playing with his toys, and his bedtime milk. We could put another bed in there. He so wanted to be friends with you. That's why he showed himself to you. When he feels safe with people he shows them his animal form."

There was a pleading look in Mrs Bucket's face and Bruce replied, saying,

"Oh, eh … Jeez … I'm not sure about that. Wait until I go home and he can have his room back. I'm sure Fergal will be fine about it. Having said that, I need to speak to those two police guys and tell them where Stevie, Fergal, and Stewie have gone."

Bruce, now not in the least bit frightened, gave Godric another tickle on his silky tummy as the lion went into a deep sleep. Once Godric had lifted his head back he began snoring very loudly, and slowly disappeared into thin air. Then a smiling Bruce went inside the house to talk to the detective police constable.

Chapter 16

Stevie could only gaze in horror as a creature slowly rose out of the black sand and dragged him along to the sea. He wondered if it was one of those legendary black mermaids … one of the nightmare kind. Her long, coarse ropes of black hair were covered in crawling sea slugs, and her dark eyes blazed red. The creature had no eyelids. Seaweed hung in swirling clumps off her bony white shoulders. She smelt of the sea. Her silver fishtail swished like a lizard's as she moved from side to side along the sand, and she only turned around now and again, licking her lips, to look at the tasty morsel she had captured.

"Let me go," he whispered to her. His throat was starting to get sore with shouting at her. His brain frantically raced in his head. Hadn't he heard that if you were trapped in sand there was something you could do?

The mermaid had stopped singing and he did not feel as tired, and was now thinking of a way to get away from her and not be her meal. What was it you did to get out of wet sand? What on earth did you do? At that moment he felt quite helpless. He had to stop her getting him into the sea.

But then there was a noise above his head and he looked up. It was Fergal flying above him, his wings flapping frantically. The bird started to swipe at the sea creature with its sharp beak, and the mermaid loosened her grip on Stevie as she tried to grab at the cormorant. Then Stevie rolled on his back and managed to push his feet forward. With this extra grip, he got up, half-wobbling in the process. Fergal, however, was still angrily pecking at the mermaid and pulling at her hair so that long tufts filled his beak, and then he began sifting them out and pulling more hair out. The mermaid screeched and headed for the sea, followed by Fergal, who was still dive-bombing her. The creature then went underwater, deeper and deeper into the sea, and Fergal lost sight of her and came back.

"You OK?"

"Yeah, you were amazing. Thank you so much. Weird … I'm not so tired now."

"I think it was her singing. It makes you go to sleep. I managed to wake up and escape. She turned her attention to you when she saw you were much larger than me, and a better meal."

"Charming. God, that was so frightening. Where's Stewie?"

"Above your head."

He was gently fluttering above him, looking concerned.

"Let's get back. Somehow I don't feel the need to check this place out, do you?"

"No," replied Fergal, guiltily thinking that if he hadn't insisted they investigate, none of this would have happened.

"What a horrible creature. She was trying to get me into the sea."

"Aye, she was trying to drown you. The black mermaids, they say, eat humans. Anyway, looks like she's gone."

"Ugh … Stewie, just the thought of it … I could have been a goner. I like sandwiches but I don't think I would want to be a Sand Witch's lunch. C'mon, let's get out of here. Hang on … There's something wrapped round my toe. I can't shake it off. It feels like rope. Ouch. It doesn't half hurt. Help me. Get it off it me."

Stevie kicked at it, but it only resulted in something large becoming stuck to his foot. He wiggled his big toe, but there was so much sand over his foot he couldn't see what it was. Whatever it was it wouldn't budge. Then the skin of his toe cut into something and his foot was starting to burn with the pain ...

"Ouch. What is that? I can't get it off my toe. It's so sharp."

Fergal helped him by pecking away at the sand and getting to what looked like a length of sturdy rope, which was wrapped quite firmly around Stevie's big toe. As a large object began to surface the rope snapped, freeing Stevie's foot, much to his relief. As he rubbed his sore foot he watched Stewie and Fergal dig out the strange object with their beaks and hand feathers. Finally they succeeded, and all three of them looked at the strange object in surprise.

It was a rusty blue tin trunk.

"What's it doing here? Blast. It's locked. I can't open it," said Stevie, as he wrestled without success with the wet, rusty lock.

"It might be treasure," said Fergal, his beak quivering at the thought of that.

"Well, we're not opening it here. That mermaid might bring back some of her mates. I don't want to be their late supper."

"Oh no! I hadn't thought of that. Let's get going," replied Fergal, and gulped. Stevie awkwardly carried the slippery, wet trunk as the three of them hurriedly made their way back to the cave leading to the house. But Stevie, unlike the other two, who were flying low about his head, was having difficulty, as his feet kept sinking into the wet sand while he walked with the cumbersome object.

Chapter 17

The hairpin bends were hair-raising as Wallace and Henrik were flung from side to side in their carriage. Where was Myra's carriage going? They had never seen this prehistoric-looking place before. Wallace and Henrik's driver had caught sight of her carriage and now, with vigour and determination and his teeth clenched, he gripped the reins firmly with his head down as his horse raced nearer and nearer to her.

Myra had spotted them and was now screaming at her carriage driver to go faster. But her horse was weary, scarred from cruel whip marks on its body, and finally, with exhaustion, the animal's worn-out legs buckled and the carriage fell forward. The horse released itself and, with new-found freedom, galloped off, despite calls from the carriage driver to stop.

"That's it. We've got her, sir," shouted Henrik, as he caught this scene from a distance. He was excitedly feeling an embarrassing urge to start laughing, and had only stopped with the aid of his handkerchief pressed against his mouth.

As their carriage raced up to Myra's, the driver stood beside it. They climbed down and looked around.

But Myra was nowhere to be seen.

"Where is she?" asked Wallace abruptly, as he desperately looked around the area.

"She went down the cliff face, sir," replied Myra's driver, who had submissively raised his hands and given himself up to the two detectives as Wallace pointed his pistol at him.

When he looked in the direction the carriage driver was now pointing, Wallace could see a grass verge. He beckoned Henrik to handcuff the carriage driver, then went to it and looked over. There was a cliff face with a sheer drop. Wide rocks were scattered around it. As he scanned his eyes over it, it was then that he spotted it – a jewelled hand hanging on to a section of the cliff face.

"Myra, give yourself up. I can see you."

"Never. Do you think I will give myself up to you, imbecile?" her high-pitched voice screamed back at him in a murderous rage.

"Well, this might not be pleasant, because I'm going to have to come down there and get you. I am not in the habit of manhandling a lady. Make it easier for yourself. Give yourself up, madam."

"Never," screeched Myra, who was now climbing further down the cliff face, almost monkey-like.

Wallace had never liked heights and felt almost dizzy as he slowly went over the grass verge and down the cliff after her, grasping wet clumps of grass and rocks with his paws. Myra, when she saw him doing this, shrieked back at him, taunting him, and began moving faster. Down and down she went, down the cliff face like a giant spider.

Wallace tried to keep up with her but he didn't have her grace, and the rocks under his feet kept crumbling. He had to grasp larger rocks with his claws for safety, and more than once he almost fell as bits of broken rock fell past him. Seeing he had not gained speed on her, she turned around and laughed with derision at his clumsy attempts to follow her, then climbed further and further down the cliff face until she was on the beach.

It was then that she saw it. A boat. An abandoned fishing boat. She laughed hysterically, lifted her black skirts, and ran across to it and dragged it further into the sea with her strong hands. Quickly, she picked up the oars and with great strength began rowing further into the sea.

Wallace half-fell down the last part of the cliff and jumped down and raced to the beach. But he was too late. The boat was now bobbing out to sea. There were no other boats to be seen. He screwed his eyes up and looked in the direction where the boat was going. He had lost her.

Frustrated, and hissing to himself, he made his way back up the cliff. His long, honey-coloured spotty tail was wagging with anger when he heard a cry. He turned around and saw a figure. It was a werewolf. It was heading his way: a pure black creature, one of the largest he had ever seen. Hunched, it charged at him, baring its yellow-fanged teeth and with saliva dripping off its twisted black lips. As he fell back, Wallace had no time to reach for his pistol.

Chapter 18

Stevie, Fergal, and Stewie were now going back up the cellar steps into the kitchen. As soon as they were met by Bruce and Miles, they explained what had happened.

"What's that?" Bruce asked.

"It was in the sand and caught on my foot. It wouldn't open."

"I think I can help you there," said Miles, who now produced a penknife from one of his deep pockets and crouched down as he began to open it. The penknife just scratched at the lock, but then he took sharp jabs at it. At first it wouldn't budge. But then there was movement and it started to open.

The lid appeared to grudgingly open, but with that motion there came an almighty roar that seemed to reverberate round the room, followed by a whistling and finally an animal-like howling, and the furniture rattled. The whole room then began to shake, and Bruce fell to the floor. The eerie howling continued, and it sounded as if there was a pack of wolves in the room. But, as the cat gulped and looked round the room, he could see that there was nothing in sight. Then there was silence.

Everyone looked at one another.

"What was that?"

No one could answer that.

Miles, slightly shaken, checked that no one was hurt and then, out of curiosity, proceeded to lift the rusty lid of the trunk. It smelt of iron. Droplets of seawater fell on his wrist. Strange, huge shapes of see-through thin jelly then began to slide out of the box and drip on the carpet, and finally disappeared into thin air.

"How weird was that?" said Bruce, shaking his head at this strange sight, but if he had known that what had just happened would now change everything he would have been more astonished. Miles had just released the trapped souls of the werewolves and monsters of the Howling Forest imprisoned by Myra Bloodvein.

Chapter 19

Wallace thought his nine lives were finally up as the werewolf charged at him. There was no cover. He did not have enough time to get his pistol. He knew he would be no match for a creature that size. There was nothing else to do. He had to fight it.

He spread out his long arms and stood raised on his feet, hoping he was looking formidable. The hair on his head rose in spiky peaks, and even his tail had become thick in size. But then something really strange happened. The ferocious-looking creature stopped in its tracks, pulled back its black head, and gave a howl that echoed around them. Then, on its hind legs, it turned around and sped off, until all that could be seen was a black outline as it headed for what appeared to be caves further along the beach.

As he scratched his head and gave a sigh of relief, Wallace stared back at it, incredulous, until nothing could be seen of the creature. Then he turned around and went to make his way back up the cliffs.

There was a shout from above him and he looked up. He could see Henrik peering down at him. He had been climbing down the cliffs and, with a final jump, landed beside him.

"You all right, sir?"

"Yes. Did you see that creature? That must have been the biggest werewolf I have ever seen."

"Yes, I did. I had my pistol aimed at it, but I didn't know if I would have managed to shoot it in time. You were very lucky. I wonder why it took off. You would have been no match for it, sir."

"I know. I thought my time was up. Heaven knows why it took off like that. But, even worse, we have lost Myra. The blasted woman took off in a boat. She was too fast getting down the cliff face, and we will never get to know where Mordeith has gone."

"We might catch up with her. She might not be experienced in a boat."

"Let's hope so. Come on. You question the carriage driver. We know where Myra lives. She might try and go back for her daughter. Let's get back there."

The two wearily climbed back up the cliff.

Chapter 20

Henrik had been right when he said Myra might not have been an experienced oarsman. Her long, thin arms struggled with the oars as she tried to go forward as fast as possible. Her attempts were clumsy and she went sideways instead. As she screamed with rage, she cursed Wallace.

How she would deal with him when she came out of the water. She would make that fur boned creature a live supper for the werewolves. He would die a long and painful death. The werewolves would kill the whole lot of them at Loch House. She wouldn't even bother getting Fergal. She would just forge his signature, but first she would need to get back to Oban, get her daughter. She wasn't bothered about her sister. Let them think she was behind it all. She could have her sister imprisoned instead of her.

Myra was a great actress. She had been on the stage. A few tears here and there, and they would think Clarinda was to blame. Yes, that's what she would do. She could then continue with her plan to marry her daughter off to a rich earl, then arrange for her daughter's husband to die. Then all the money would be hers. Fenella was, she thought, too stupid to be a problem.

Myra was so engrossed in her scheming that she did not see the mysterious lumbering shape that swam under the boat until it was too late. The huge black cat was an agile swimmer. It stretched its inky, shiny black body and looked up at the boat. It smelt human blood. It gave a smile. Then, with one of its heavy, black-clawed paws, it swiped at the underside of the boat. The force of its paw made the boat move from side to side. The cat struck again, playing with its prey, watching in amusement.

This time the boat rocked more to one side. A final strike from the cat, and the boat rolled over. The enormous cat's almond-shaped yellow eyes glinted with pleasure. The human fell out. Myra, terrified, went to swim away from the creature. She could not believe her eyes when she saw what was now staring at her. The cat's eyes were the size of the boat, and the animal continued to watch the human's wasted attempts at trying to escape from it.

It gave her gentle swipes now and again, which made Myra's long black wig uncoil and come off her head, revealing her scrawny, bald head. The cat seized this strange black coiled hair. It played with the long strands and bit into the thick clumps. It did not like the taste of the perfume and powder, so it spat bits of hair out.

The cat was now bored, and blamed Myra for the strange taste on its tongue. It angrily chased after her, but Myra, a keen swimmer, had swum a distance from it. But because of the sheer size of the creature it easily caught up with her. Then, with one of its paws, it grabbed hold of her, holding her to its face to have one last look at her. Her face displeased it.

The last things Myra saw were the sabre-toothed jaws of the devil cat as it popped her in its mouth and swallowed her up. The Marchioness of Bute had been right. The mysterious black cat of the sea did exist.

The cat then ripped the boat into shreds. Now happy with the destruction it had caused, it gave a satisfied stretch and swam deep into the sea, purring loudly. All that was left of Myra was her long black wig, which hung in rat's tails in the water as it bobbed on the surface. The wig eventually landed on the head of a surprised brown seal as it came up from under the water. It would only be later that the Black Cat of Bute would suffer terrible indigestion, brought on no doubt by something bad it had eaten earlier.

Chapter 21

Nobody ever knew what happened to Myra Bloodvein. It was as if she had vanished into thin air. It disturbed Wallace Whiskerman. It was rare for him not to catch his villains and, of course, he had now lost any hope of finding Mordeith. This would be a real problem, as the warlock would continue with his assassination attempts against the royal family.

Wallace had found out through an informant that Mordeith believed himself to be the true king of England. This was due to an indiscretion on the part of William IV, which had resulted in Mordeith's birth. But his birth had never been acknowledged and the warlock had been kept hidden in various orphanages until he had grown up and learnt the truth. He had then vowed revenge on all members of the royal family.

Clarinda, Myra's sister, now had full custody of Myra's daughter. Fenella did not seem to miss her mother and had slowly changed from a spoilt young lady to a thoroughly nice girl. Clarinda had taught her to treat animals with respect and all her long-suffering pets were now living much happier lives, supervised by Clarinda.

Wallace Whiskerman had, after a thorough check of the island, returned to London with his men. It had been established that Miles had indeed set free the souls of the werewolves and monsters. Howly Island would continue to have werewolves and monsters living on it, but they were no longer a threat to the locals.

The werewolves that had been killed had been given proper, Christian burials by their families as a mark of respect.

The werewolves in Howly Forest were no longer forced by Myra to kill people. Wallace was satisfied that they would no longer be a threat to humans. The creatures stayed in the vast Howling Forest and kept to themselves. They now had their freedom and would keep well away from people … unless that is, of course, any overcurious human ventured into their forest. If they did it would be a very stupid thing to do, because they were unlikely to be seen again.

Bruce, Stevie, and Fergal had returned to Edinburgh, but Bruce had been quite sad. This was because when he had gone to see Callie McFarrell before going home, a formidable-looking ginger cat with handlebar whiskers, dressed in a black suit and waistcoat, had been in the bakery instead of her. The cat informed Bruce rather brusquely that he was Callie McFarrell's uncle. Then, looking disapprovingly at Bruce, he told him that Callie was out with her aunt, buying her wedding trousseau for her forthcoming wedding. When Bruce told Stevie later about this, Stevie had said,

"Cheer up, Bruce. You'll meet someone just as nice."

Bruce had replied half-heartedly,

"Will I? It's just that I would like to have seen her before she went away. Do you know, I never even noticed she was wearing an engagement ring. How stupid was I? I bet she wouldn't have looked at me." The little cat gave a deep sigh full of self-pity and looked up mournfully at Stevie and shrugged his shoulders.

"Of course she would have. Don't be daft. Never mind. Look on the bright side. Weren't you glad we got away from Howly Island?"

"Yeah, but Fergal will expect us to come and visit now and again," replied Bruce, pulling a face.

"Oh, crikey. I hadn't thought of that. Come on, let's forget about it for the moment. My mum will be giving me earache if we don't get the buffet food sorted. Come on."

Bruce gave a small smile and followed Stevie into the kitchen.

The boys had arrived home after Mr Beavis. He had returned on the first train, and had not waited for the trio. After a terse farewell he had been off as quickly as his checked trouser legs could carry him.

Fergal had then gone back with Stevie and Bruce temporarily to get the last of his things, but had decided Howly Island would be his home. Stewie and Mr and Mrs Bucket would remain at Loch House and would be employed there for the rest of their lives. Mr and Mrs Bucket were also instructed by Fergal to find a good bookkeeper. Even the vampire bats appeared to have disappeared into thin air, and locals had slowly started to come back to the island.

Chapter 22

It was now Halloween in the Rump household.

Stevie Rump's parents, Christine and Max, had been informed by Wallace Whiskerman that Stevie, Bruce, and Fergal had been a great help to him in chasing villains. Stevie's parents had not been happy at first, but the charm of the cheetah smoothed things over, which was fortunate for the worried trio.

Today Bruce was busy decorating an enormous chocolate cake with a brown and orange marzipan spider as the centrepiece. Carefully he piped whirls of white icing over the cake to make his delicate cobwebs. Stevie sat on a stool watching him. Now and again he sneaked bits of melted chocolate whirls and popped them into his mouth. Christine Rump had organised a Halloween party to welcome the orphaned children, who were due to arrive in the house in less than two hours' time.

"Hey, Bruce, did you see the newspaper today?"

"No, why?"

"Wallace Whiskerman is on the front page. He's getting an award for outstanding bravery for saving Queen Victoria's life. Someone tried to assassinate her. He single-handedly caught the assassin. The paper says the assassin was a warlock called Mordeith. See, there is a sketch, and doesn't he half look evil?" Stevie lifted the picture up to Bruce to show him the warlock.

Bruce shuddered and gave a nervous meow, and continued piping the cake. The newspaper sketch of the warlock looked very menacing indeed. The assassin had an enormous long head, with a wide bent nose covered in lumpy pustules. His eyes were very dark, almost black, and slanted at the corners. His nose came to a sharp point and almost touched his top lip, which was much smaller than his extremely thick bottom lip.

"The police had been looking for him. How glad am I we never got to meet him. Oh, look, look ... See, there is a picture of Wallace on the front page." Bruce nodded back but didn't look as he piped the chocolate. Stevie continued to read the paper and looked back at the front page. Then he lifted the front page of the newspaper again and held the cover towards Bruce, saying,

"Don't you think Wallace looks cool?"

"Wow. Yeah, he sure does. Man, I wish I spoke and looked like him," Bruce replied, looking and giving a slight purr as he piped more iced cobwebs round the huge cake. Telltale signs of the fresh cream he had been gorging on were dotted on his white chin.

Stevie continued to read the rest of the article.

"It said Wallace happened to be a bystander when Queen Victoria was coming out of her carriage at Marble Arch. Wallace stopped the warlock by throwing his jacket over him in the split second he was aiming a gun at the Queen, even before her bodyguard noticed. In fact, Wallace jumped on top of the assassin and grabbed his gun."

Impressively, the photograph of Wallace had him dressed in top hat and tails, with a yellow and orange spotted handkerchief in his breast pocket, which matched his fur. He had grown a thin black moustache that curled up at the ends, which had not managed to cover his brilliant white pointed teeth. These were displayed proudly to the camera as he held the gold medal with vigour in his yellow-spotted right paw. His wife was beside him, dressed in a pink cloak: a small, female cheetah with round brown eyes, who was roughly a foot shorter. Her auburn hair was coiled in a bun. She was round-faced, and wearing what looked like a rather large black hat. This was covered in a collection of brightly coloured flowers and fruit. The black-and-white photograph captured the couple linking arms with each other as they proudly came out of Buckingham Palace. It was difficult to judge which of them had the whiter teeth.

"What a man," said Bruce as Stevie replaced the newspaper on the dresser.

"Yeah, he was. A bit like a posh version of Ethan. That Henrik was funny, though, wasn't he? Always laughing. Even when he was trying to be serious he would break into a laugh. I don't think he could help it. I think hyenas always laugh like that. I'm sure I read something about that somewhere."

"Oh, do they? How weird is that?" replied Bruce, pursing his lips as he proceeded to cream a tricky corner of the cake.

Turning their faces to the door they could hear Stevie's mother's voice in the hallway they looked at each other and knew that they now had to concentrate on making Stevie's mother's party ready and stop chatting. The party had to be a success and they didn't want to let Stevie's mother down. They also hoped it would help Fergal take his mind off the terrible way his uncle had died.

Her hopes of filling the home had come to fruition. Orphans from all over England were now coming to the home. More homes were being built, and Christine carefully scrutinised them and the staff. The Rump house was now filled with warmth and love, with not an unhappy ghostly apparition in sight.

Well, apart from one ...

Bruce's friend.

The little cat had not yet told the others about it. He was trying to decide how he would tell them. The problem was that his friend wanted to live with them. But how on earth was he going to ask Christine Rump if Godric could come to stay? He decided to wait until after the party and get her on her own. He would win her over with some of his special iced fudge cake. He had delicately decorated it with tiny billowing blue butterflies crafted from sugar.

In deep thought he shook his head. He decided that yes, that's what he would do. His friend had promised to keep out of the way until he had asked Christine Rump. Surely she would be OK about it. After all, she got on well with him. She was bound to like his friend, wasn't she?

The Rump house was gloriously decorated. Fergal had made paper skeletons and flew around the room sticking them on the ceiling, so they swayed whenever a door was opened. Candied pink snails, jellied slugs, and coconut jellied eyeballs filled glass jars placed in rows on the wooden kitchen dresser. Plates of iced shortbread biscuits shaped as ghosts lay in rows on deep plates. There was even a Halloween pudding, which was a bit like fruit cake. Both Fergal and Bruce's cooking and baking expertise had produced amazing creations. The whole house smelt of chocolate, cinnamon, and honey, which wafted deliciously through every room in the house.

Bruce and Fergal had spent all day in preparation for the party, with Stevie assisting them. It was to mark all the new boys and girls coming to live at the home and to make them feel welcome and loved. Presents had been placed in every bedroom, all lovingly wrapped by Christine and Max Rump. Pumpkin soup was to be warmed up later. Assorted sandwiches, pies and cakes, and a glass cake stand covered with Victorian tartlets and custard patties decorated the dining room table. The sheer weight of the food made the table look slightly lopsided. A huge trifle covered in jellied fruit stood in between some plates of miniature pork pies. It was a feast fit for a king.

Bruce finally finished piping the final side of the chocolate cake. It was to be the centrepiece of the table. He gazed admiringly at his creation and smiled, satisfied it was perfect. Fergal had done an amazing job on the delicate tartlets, which lay on handmade lace doilies, and on all the other fine pastries, which were laid side by side next to the brightly coloured trifle in its huge glass bowl engraved with swans. He placed the monster of a cake on a heavy glass cake stand, and struggled with the sheer weight of it as he went to take it into the dining room.

"How beautiful, Bruce. Well done. Here, give it to me. I'll take it into the dining room," said Christine as she came into the room. She was a tall, attractive woman, with blue eyes and a long, thin face. She was wearing a starched high-collared blue dress with a slight bustle. Her long wavy brown hair was held up with a collection of pins in a loose bun. But there was something wrong. Her eyes were shining, and it looked as if she had been crying.

"Mrs Rump, are you all right?" Bruce looked up at her, surprised and concerned. His right paw jerked as he held the cake, ready to comfort her.

"Yes, dear, I'm fine, Bruce. Oh, I think I heard the door knocker. Can you get it for me?" She took the cake from him and made to go out of the door.

"Eh, yes, are you sure you're OK? Sorry, I didn't hear it."

"Mum, what's wrong?" asked a worried Stevie as he placed one of his long arms on his mother's right shoulder. He was starting to get very worried by the look on her face.

"Stevie, I'm fine. Honestly, I'm fine. Bruce, please, *please*, can you answer the door?"

Stevie and Bruce looked at each other, both extremely concerned. It was obvious that Stevie's mother had been crying.

"Whatever is the matter with her?" But Bruce did as she said and went out of the kitchen. He wondered why she hadn't gone to the door first, as she would have been the nearest there, and was still hoping there was nothing wrong with her.

"Mum?"

"Stevie, darling, something wonderful is about to happen."

Stevie followed her into the dining room as she laid the cake on the table. Christine Rump then took her handkerchief out of her apron pocket and sniffed into it. Tears were now falling down her cheeks.

"Mum?"

"Let me get my breath and I'll tell you," she said, crying and half-laughing at the same time as she hugged him.

Chapter 23

Bruce went into the draughty, tiled hallway. It was freezing cold. He shivered. He rubbed his shoulders with his paws and coughed slightly. As he looked up, he saw the brightly coloured diamond-panelled glass door was wide open. A solitary figure had entered through it. Whoever they were, they were short and well-rounded.

It was a female tabby cat with a tiny check purple bonnet tightly placed on her round head in between her ears, with a lavender strap under her chin. The figure was wearing a worn thin wool dress in a grey and black check, and black laced-up boots. She looked up at him and put down the wicker basket she was carrying. There was a large tapestry case beside her.

It was his Aunt Lucy staring at him with her saucer-sized green eyes, purring softly.

Bruce didn't have a chance to speak. The plump feline figure charged at him, wrapped him in her warm arms, and continued to smother him in dozens of fishy kisses. But this was too much for a shell-shocked Bruce, who started to cry. His Aunt Lucy was smiling, and she stroked his striped head and cuddled him. Then she softly kissed him on both cheeks. And then, after taking out a handkerchief from out of one of her lace sleeves, she delicately wiped his eyes as tears of joy now poured down his face.

Fergal and Stevie couldn't believe it when Christine told him Bruce's Aunt Lucy was in the hallway.

"I'll go and see him."

"Not yet, Fergal. Leave them a while."

"How did they find her?" asked Stevie.

"Those wonderful Dog Pirates, Ethan and Saros, found her. They are in the parlour. Do you know they never gave up looking for her? Finally they found her on a remote island in the Caribbean, along with other escaped prisoners who had been slaves of the Sea Witches of Glendowwer. The prisoners were stranded and couldn't get off the island. There were no mermaids or sea mammals to send word of where they were. It was a primitive place. The Dog Pirates found them by accident. We never told Bruce they were still looking for her. We didn't want to get his hopes up."

"Wow … You mean Ethan and Saros are here?"

"Yes, Stevie, eating a plate of salted beef sandwiches, some pies, and drinking some ale. I think they'll be quite happy by now. You can go and see them now. Leave Bruce and his aunt for a while. They will have a lot to talk about. I'll just take some more of the food from the kitchen into the dining room."

Stevie and Fergal raced into the parlour. Their adventures with the Dog Pirates on the Island of Glendowwer had never left their minds. The hugged the Dog Pirates, and began talking excitedly to them.

But then it happened – a blood-curdling scream from Christine Rump – and everyone rushed into the dining room, fearing the worst. Ethan the Rhodesian ridgeback and Saros the Rottweiler charged ahead first, both drawing their cutlasses. Facing them was an enormous, golden-maned lion tucking into the specially decorated spider chocolate cake that had graced the table. Parts of the cake were now on the floor, and wet milk chocolate dripped off the lion's face as the creature lay sprawled across the floor. His huge velvet honey-coloured nose was covered in chocolate. He looked rather guilty as the large decorated marzipan spider that had been on the cake slid off one of his whiskers into a chocolate puddle on the ground.

After gulping and finishing by swallowing half the chocolate cake he then began to look around at everyone with his enormous yellow eyes and tried purring loudly. Then he rolled on to his back, showing his luxuriant golden tummy. He hoped they would all be his friend. Then he gave a very loud belch.

Bruce stuttered at first, tried to ward off purr hiccups, and said sheepishly,

"Oh, Jeez … er … er … Everyone, meet my pal Godric. He's a lion. He's, er … a sort of ghost. We made friends a while ago at Howly Island. He lives with the Buckets. He belonged to Remus McFetrich at Loch House … kinda seems to have followed me here.

He's been very lonely and just wants to be pals. Can he stay a while, Mrs Rump? He won't be any trouble, honest."

And with that, the lion looked up at Bruce. He gave a deep, contented purr, and stood up and shook himself. After spraying everyone with liquid chocolate, he went over to Bruce and planted a slobbery kiss on his head. Then he padded over to Christine Rump, jumped up, earnestly placed his huge paws on her chest, looked deep into her eyes, and gave a drum-like purr. This friendly action, unfortunately, only caused her to scream again and to fall into a deep faint. Only a lace handkerchief drenched with lavender would revive her a half an hour later.

And so that was that. The trio had a new friend, who they will continue their adventures with. But they would face their worst adversary yet when they came face to face with the legendary snow beast terror.

But, of course, that is another story to tell.

Printed in Great Britain
by Amazon